HOW TO LOSE A JOB

A Kate Williams Mystery

Becky Bartness

iUniverse, Inc.
New York   Bloomington

How to Lose a Job

A Kate Williams Mystery

Copyright © 2009 by Becky Bartness

This is a work of fiction. All of the characters, names, incidents, organizations, and dialogue in this novel are either the products of the author's imagination or are used fictitiously.

iUniverse books may be ordered through booksellers or by contacting:

iUniverse
1663 Liberty Drive
Bloomington, IN 47403
www.iuniverse.com
1-800-Authors (1-800-288-4677)

Because of the dynamic nature of the Internet, any Web addresses or links contained in this book may have changed since publication and may no longer be valid. The views expressed in this work are solely those of the author and do not necessarily reflect the views of the publisher, and the publisher hereby disclaims any responsibility for them.

ISBN: 978-0-595-50000-0 (pbk)
ISBN: 978-0-595-49709-6 (cloth)
ISBN: 978-0-595-61336-6 (ebk)

Printed in the United States of America

iUniverse rev. date: 3/6/09

Chapter One

I looked out my office window, which afforded a fine view into the adjacent building. The occupant directly opposite me, a mid-fiftyish, short, balding man, waved and smiled. I didn't know what the man did for a living, but whatever it was, it was not labor intensive. We made eye contact whenever I looked out my window because he was perpetually looking at me. If his desk was facing the window so he would inevitably look into my office whenever he raised his head, I could understand him. But his desk was facing in the opposite direction, so he had to make a real effort to see me.

I lowered the metal louvered shades on my window with a bang. Let him find something else to do.

I shoved a case file off my scratched metal desk with my foot, being careful not to scuff my Manolo Blahnik shoe, then put my feet up on the desk and leaned back in my fake leather chair.

After plucking a blond hair off the lapel of my St. John's jacket, I closed my eyes and sighed contentedly.

By objective standards I had taken a step down in the legal profession. Less than a year ago I was one of the top criminal law attorneys in Chicago but made the decision to move to Phoenix, Arizona, in search of a more rational lifestyle. I was working eighty-hour weeks in Chicago with, needless to say, no social life and a law partner more interested in my billable hours than my mental health. A trip to an Arizona dude ranch changed my perspective; I discovered there was more to life than the law and a large income.

I was not able to abandon the legal profession completely, since it was the only income-earning talent I had, and, after all, I needed to support myself, a large purebred dog (although no one, including me, seemed to know which breed) named Ralph that I adopted at the dude ranch, and about a hundred and fifty pairs of shoes and an equal number of handbags.

Once I made the decision to move to Phoenix, I had no problem getting a job at the Maricopa County Attorney's office in the major felony division. The recently elected county attorney, Stan Rantwist, seemed thrilled to have me on board.

I figured the switch from the defense side to the prosecutor's side wouldn't be difficult. In fact, it might be a pleasant change. For years I had represented folks charged with crimes. Some were innocent, but most were most decidedly guilty of something, if not the crime for which they were charged. I'd struggled in the hardscrabble world of private practice long enough. From my point of view, prosecutors had it easy; only one client (the State) to deal with; support staff up the kazoo, including a legion of detectives and paralegals; expert resources like a crime labs and CSI personnel, a steady paycheck. It was going to be a piece of cake.

Two weeks into the job I was sincerely enjoying my new position and my (more or less) nine-to-five workday. But then so far my case load was light, and I had been largely left alone.

My idyllic situation was about to change.

I heard a loud knock, and the door crashed open. MJ Polowski, my newly assigned paralegal, entered the room staggering under the weight of an enormous stack of files.

I growled a sarcasm laden, "Come in," hoping to make the point that I did not like unannounced crashing and entering.

I'd been introduced to MJ the day before. The extent of our conversation was "Hello, I'm Kate Williams" (me) and "Whatever" (MJ).

MJ (short for Mary Jane, a name which did not fit her in the least) is mid fortyish, but was not giving in to middle age without a fight. Her long frizzy hair is an unnatural shade of orange with red highlights, and her arms are covered with an amazing range, both as to color and content, of tattoos. Equally impressive are her body piercings which, from her neck up alone, include three studs in each ear and one in her upper lip and, new today, a nose ring. She was wearing a hot pink miniskirt made out of some kind of shiny material, Doc Marten boots, iridescent green knee-highs, and a white tank top emblazoned with a black skull. She was braless, thus affording a fine view to all of her nipple rings.

She plopped the files on my desk and threw herself into a chair.

The chair sagged and groaned, not because MJ was overly heavy (although she could stand to lose a few pounds), but because the chair was old and perilously close to giving up and giving out.

"Your new cases," MJ announced, waving at the files with one hand and ineffectually pushing her unruly hair out of her eyes with the other.

"New nose ring?" I asked.

"Yeah. And it hurts like a bitch. I may need the rest of the day off."

I ignored this last comment and picked up a file from the stack MJ had just delivered. "Anything good in these?" I asked.

"How the hell should I know? It was all I could do to carry them from the file room to your office. Now you want me to read them, too? That's not part of my job description."

Some things never changed. Throughout my working life I had always managed to end up with the MJs of the world working for me: low on ambition, big on attitude.

"In fact, it *is* your job to read them. As my paralegal, it is your responsibility to summarize the contents of each of these files for me."

"At my salary, you're lucky I show up in the morning. Summarize your own damn files."

I restrained myself from giving the ring in MJ's nose a tweak. I would … I *would* … stay calm in my new stress-free environment.

Smiling sweetly, I lowered my feet to the floor and leaned over my desk toward her.

"Have file summaries on my desk tomorrow morning, or I will personally see to it that you no longer need to endure your low salary, or any salary for that matter."

MJ's eyes narrowed. She clenched her fists and flexed impressive biceps. (MJ worked out.) "Empty threats don't impress me. A salary raise would impress me."

"What makes you think it's an empty threat? I spent fourteen years in Chicago successfully defending some of the most dangerous felons in the country. I know some guys who could make your life *very* difficult."

We stared at each other. MJ blinked first.

She heaved herself up, grabbed the files, and stomped out. Intent on getting in the last word, she said over her shoulder, "You're a sick fuck, you know that?" Then she slammed the door for emphasis.

I learned early in my career that the only effective way to deal with employees like MJ was strategic use of threats, and heaven knows I had experience dealing with employees like MJ. I had gotten so good at the threat thing that most of the employees in my Chicago firm had taken to wearing body armor by the time I left. Even my partner wore a helmet on Mondays.

I leaned over and picked up the file I'd kicked to the floor earlier and flipped it open.

Skimming the contents, I gleaned that one Larry Larkin had been arrested by a sheriff's deputy on Central Avenue and Third Street, sans pants, at five thirty in the afternoon; just in time for rush hour. He was booked and charged with felony assault and battery.

The charges were confusing. While a charge of assault made some sense, because an assault only required that a victim be placed in fear of immediate bodily injury, a charge of battery required that the victim be physically touched in some way, and the police report didn't reflect the occurrence of any contact with a victim. In fact, the report didn't even include the names of any victims. On the contrary; the people driving by had seemed to enjoy the diversion and treated Larkin to wolf whistles, kissing noises, and offers of sunscreen and Viagra.

I checked the file to see if he had prior convictions that justified the heightened charge but could find none.

Perhaps the charging division had been a bit overzealous, or had simply not reviewed the file carefully enough. I made a mental note to discuss the charges against Mr. Larkin the next time I met with County Attorney Rantwist.

I glanced at the clock. It was four forty-five. In fifteen minutes the rush to the elevator would begin with seven hundred employees of the county attorney's office simultaneously trying to squeeze into the single small elevator standing between them and freedom.

I decided to wait out the mass exodus. By six o'clock the building would be pretty much empty, and I would have a clear shot at the elevator.

I closed my eyes and sat back in my chair again, and was considering my restaurant options for dinner when, once again, a knock sounded at the door, after which it immediately opened.

"Come in," I muttered sarcastically, annoyed at being disturbed before I could decide between Mexican and Italian food.

"Ms. Williams, Could I have a moment of your time?"

I cracked one eye open and identified the speaker as my investigator, Marcus John Martinez-O'Reilly Ramirez. I'd met him yesterday at the same time I met MJ. The story was that, to avoid confusion between Marcus John and MJ (although I found it hard to believe how any confusion between the sartorially elegant Marcus John and MJ could exist on any level), Marcus John was at first dubbed JM by the office staff. Confusion still ran rampant, however, so now Marcus John was simply, if inexplicably, referred to as Sam.

Sam went to the chair recently vacated by MJ and stared at it suspiciously. He brushed the seat off before gingerly sitting on the chair's edge.

Having achieved a seated position entailing minimal contact with the chair, he brushed an imaginary piece of lint off his navy trousers, then folded his hands neatly in his lap and looked at me expectantly.

I wondered if I'd scheduled a meeting with Sam and forgotten about it, but a quick scan of my memory bank indicated I had not. Clearly, however, something was required of me to get a conversation going.

"You may proceed," I said.

This seemed to work.

"Well, as you know, it is this office's policy that a deputy prosecutor and his or her investigator meet at least once a week to discuss their caseload."

Sam looked at me. He appeared to be waiting for a signal affirming that this was my understanding as well.

I nodded obligingly.

"Since you have been here for two weeks and we have not discussed our cases, I believe this policy has been breached."

I stared at Sam for several uncomfortable (for him) seconds. He shifted in his seat nervously. Since, perched as he was, there was very little seat on which to shift, he nearly fell on the floor.

"Well, Sam, since I have only handled five cases since I started here and all of them pled out, and because you were not assigned to my team until yesterday, I saw no reason for a meeting."

Sam was not deterred by logic. "Michelle in filing said MJ brought several files up to you today, and you talked to MJ here in your office. I believe I am entitled to a meeting as well."

Were those tears in Sam's eyes?

There was always a Michelle in filing. She could be a Sally or a Mary; the name didn't matter. Her function was the same everywhere: to serve as a conduit of information, rumor, and innuendo and, if the opportunity presented itself, to create conflict and cause angst for sheer entertainment value.

"Yes, MJ brought in some files, then she left with them. I told her I needed summaries of each of them prior to my review."

Sam looked doubtfully at me. "You told MJ to do case summaries ... and she said she would?"

I nodded even though MJ didn't exactly *agree* to anything. It was more like she succumbed to threats.

His eyes narrowed with suspicion. "Did you give her a raise?"

My patience, admittedly anorexic under normal circumstances, was running thin. "No," I said tersely.

Sam's expression turned into one of awe. "Did she hit you?" he asked.

"No. I believe she wanted to, though."

"She'll probably show up tomorrow with another tattoo or piercing. She always does that when she's mad or upset," commented Sam.

I figured MJ must be mad or upset a lot.

"Yesterday she had a fight with her boyfriend, Mitchie. That's why she got the nose ring."

"I really don't want to hear about MJ's coping strategies," I said flatly. "I don't care if she shows up tomorrow with a bone through her nose and a tattoo of Johnny Depp on her forehead."

"God, I love Johnny Depp," sighed Sam.

The conversation had taken an unexpected turn.

Sam gazed soulfully at an empty space above my head, likely engaging in a Johnny Depp fantasy.

"Are we through here?" I asked brusquely.

Sam appeared to bookmark his place in Depp-land and reluctantly re-focused on the real world after evidencing some initial confusion, probably as to whether I was asking if he was through with his Johnny Depp musings (the answer being no) or our meeting (which had pretty much run its course).

He uncrossed his legs and stood. He repeated the nonexistent lint brushing procedure on his pants and carefully adjusted his paisley tie. Then he saluted me sharply and departed, leaving behind a scent suspiciously like Shalimar.

I looked at the clock again. It was only five. My exchange with Sam had taken less than ten minutes. It had seemed to last much longer.

I heard the distant thunder of hundreds of government employees' feet heading toward the nearest exit at top speed. I hoped this signaled the end of unannounced intrusions into my office. I considered my options with regard to the latter. Even if I locked the door, I knew MJ, Sam, and the county attorney all had keys, and that was three too many if I was going to have any privacy at all.

I glared at the door and wondered if I could find anyone in the tunnels of bureaucracy who could change the lock for me.

A knock sounded at the door, and again it immediately opened. Alan White, Rantwist's assistant and the number-two man in the office, came in.

"Enter," I grumbled rhetorically.

Alan White was a middle-aged, skinny, sharp-nosed man of medium height. He was notorious for his lack of both fashion sense and personal hygiene. Today he wore a brown suit and black shoes. A stretch of beige socks appeared between his pant cuffs and shoe tops. His tie had probably been blue originally, but now it was so badly stained that it looked kind of plaid.

I met Alan early on in the hiring process and immediately disliked him. Unfortunately, the county attorney seldom appeared without Alan at his side, so it was hard to avoid him if you wanted any face time with Rantwist. Alan had been second in command in the four previous administrations as well, and rumor was that he kept his job only because he knew where all the bones were buried. Some even went so far as to say that Alan was the real power behind the scenes. I didn't give Alan credit for being that smart, though. He was more the county attorney's spy than his advisor. Alan had a habit of sneaking around and listening to other people's conversations. He was probably so accustomed to functioning as a master spy that, even though he had no reason to sneak into my office since he'd already announced his arrival, he looked around nervously and half-closed the door before sidling into the room.

He soundlessly moved across the floor and sat down in the chair previously occupied by MJ, then Sam.

I was beginning to understand why the chair was on its last legs. This was definitely a high traffic area.

Alan's thin lips were perpetually fixed in a half smile. His lips barely moved when he spoke.

He mumbled something.

"Pardon?"

He mumbled again, slightly louder than before.

I leaned across my desk to get nearer. "Still can't hear you. Try again."

Alan dutifully tried again. This time I was able to make out the gist of what he was saying.

"County Attorney Rantwist would like to see you in his office, if you have a minute."

Even though his tone was obsequiously polite, he managed to convey that this was an order rather than a request.

"I'll be happy to talk to Stan."

Alan flinched when I referred to the county attorney by his first name.

"You should tell Stan to just give me a call next time," I said sweetly. "I'm sure you have better things to do than play messenger boy."

I was pretty sure he didn't.

Alan's half smile disappeared for a split second. "I need to go over our protocol procedures before we go up to the County Attorney's office," he continued prissily.

I drew a blank on this one. "Protocol? What kind of protocol?"

"In recognition of the dignity of the office of the County Attorney, we have put into effect certain protocol requirements applicable to a person or persons appearing before the County Attorney."

This came as a surprise. I'd met with Stan Rantwist a couple of times before I was hired. He didn't seem the type to impose rules of protocol.

"Is this something new?" I asked.

Alan cleared his throat softly and glanced behind him. "I notice that at times the staff fails to evidence appropriate respect for the office of the County Attorney. At my suggestion, the County Attorney has seen fit to put certain rules in place to remind employees of the importance of his sacred office."

The man wasn't the pope, for God's sake. He was an elected official. *Sacred office* under the circumstances was an oxymoron.

I figured Alan must have dreamed up the idea of an established protocol in order to buttress his own importance by association.I wasn't in the mood to argue the point with him, however. I didn't want to do anything to prolong this meeting. I would play along, provided Alan's rules of protocol didn't require that I wear peculiar clothing or kiss Stan's ring.

Alan, unaware of my mutinous thoughts, proceeded to outline the rules.

"First, you must sign in with the County Attorney's secretary, Beth. Beth will then contact the County Attorney if, and only if, he is not already in a meeting or on the phone. The County Attorney may then, but is not required to, notify you through his secretary that he will see you."

I liked these rules. I thought they should apply across the board to all attorneys on staff.

I nodded seriously to indicate that, thus far, I was on board.

"Next, before you enter the County Attorney's office, please remove your shoes. The County Attorney does not like his wood floors scratched."

Okay, this was a bit unusual. But then, remembering a previous law partner who made his secretary wear a hairnet in the office due to an abnormal fear of stray hairs, I rationalized that it wasn't *that* unusual.

"I think I understand all the rules. Do I need to sign an acknowledgment or take a pledge now?" I hope Alan got the hint that there'd better not be any more rules.

"No, no need for anything like that," said Alan, although he looked as though he thought both an acknowledgment and a pledge were darn good ideas. No doubt the next person in the office subjected to Alan's rules presentation would be required to do both.

"We may proceed now to the County Attorney's office," Alan said as he stood. "Come with me, Miss Williams."

"Ms.," I corrected automatically.

Alan did not acknowledge my correction.

I pushed my chair back, stood up, and motioned for him to go first. I'd be damned if I let him walk behind me where I couldn't see him.

Alan nodded curtly and headed toward the elevator. I followed, making rude faces behind his back, which was just the sort of behavior I feared from him had I allowed him to follow me.

We rode the elevator to the top floor without speaking, although Alan hummed atonally during the entire ascent.

The doors opened, and, with Alan once again in the lead, we walked down the long corridor to the secretary's area outside Rantwist's office. His secretary, Beth, was not at her station. No doubt she had left with the rest of the staff at five o'clock. The rules of protocol did not anticipate Beth's absence; ergo, compliance with the rules was not possible.

Alan hesitated at Beth's desk, unsure how to proceed.

I marched past him, rolling my eyes, and banged on Rantwist's door. I waited until I heard a responsive "Come in" before entering, thus complying with at least the spirit of the rules of protocol.

I entered Rantwist's office and quickly closed the door before Alan could follow me in. Rantwist was seated behind an ornately carved mahogany desk in a large, deep red leather chair. Neither the desk nor the chair was standard issue for government employees, most of whom had gray metal desks and plastic green faux leather chairs like mine.

Rantwist was on the phone but motioned for me to sit down.

I sat in a comfortable leather club chair facing the county attorney's desk.

He was engaged in a conversation with someone he referred to as "Jimmy," the substance of which was an in-depth discussion of a recent golf game between the two.

Since it was July, it was still light out. The late afternoon sun streamed through the window behind Rantwist and surrounded him like a halo, but that's where the resemblance to anything angelic ended. His nose was reminiscent of a pig's snout, a resemblance that did not go unmentioned among the staff, behind his back of course. He had deep-set blue-black eyes which were further emphasized by dark, bushy eyebrows. Overall, though, the combination of his facial features was dramatic, an effect only partially offset by the absurdity of his hairstyle. Rantwist was one of those deluded men who wrap over-long side hair around their balding heads, convinced they have the world fooled. I noticed that today the hair stretched over Rantwist's bald spot had separated into greasy strands, one of which had slid out of formation and hung to his shoulder. Since Rantwist apparently believed that no one else realized he was bald, and since I had no intention of being the one to break the news that his secret was out, I forbore from bringing the matter to his attention.

Rantwist's discussion of the thirteenth hole finally wound down, and he and Jimmy signed off.

"Kate," boomed Rantwist. "Good to see y'all."

Rantwist boomed a lot. His quasi-southern accent was an affectation, though. He'd been born and raised and lived in Massachusetts until he moved to Arizona seven years ago.

"Alan, why don't you take a seat too."

I jerked my head around and saw Alan standing behind me. I hadn't heard the door open. How did the man do that?

Alan sidled over to a straight-backed chair located to the right and behind me.

"Kate, thanks for coming up here on such short notice. Alan didn't bother you with that crap about protocol, did he?"

I turned and glared at Alan. Alan's permanent half smile was unchanged.

"As a matter of fact..." I started to say.

"A little 'welcome to the gang' humor, I'm afraid," Alan interrupted smoothly. "I apologize, Kate. Apparently you didn't get the joke."

"Your wit is so obscure as to be nonexistent," I muttered.

"Pardon me? I didn't quite catch that," said Alan.

"I said I look forward to more such witty expressions of camaraderie."

I had a few witty expressions of my own in mind.

"Good, good," said Rantwist. "Nothing like a bit of fun to help build teamwork. Oh, by the way, if you don't mind, Kate, could you take your shoes off before you come in next time? I don't want the wood floors scratched."

I looked down and saw that both Alan and Rantwist were in stockinged feet.

I suddenly missed Chicago.

"Kate, I asked you up here to find out how things are going for you so far. Is everything working out okay?"

"Actually, I haven't had much to do during the last two weeks. However, judging by the number of files MJ brought up to my office this afternoon, the honeymoon is over, and the real work begins."

Rantwist's grin widened. "I figured you'd be settled in by now and were ready to handle a normal workload. Your new cases should keep you busy but hopefully won't be too much for you. Did you have a chance to look at any of them yet?"

"Not yet. I will start once MJ provides me with case summaries," I said.

Rantwist looked surprised. "You asked MJ to do case summaries?"

I was getting tired of this reaction.

"Yes."

"Did she hit you?"

"No."

"Just wait," Rantwist chortled. "She'll either call in sick tomorrow or show up with a new tattoo or body piercing. And just to be on the safe side," he added with mock seriousness, "you may want somebody else—somebody you don't care that much about—to start your car tonight."

Maybe Alan was available.

Then I remembered the Larkin case and jumped on it as a way to turn the discussion away from MJ's bizarre coping strategies.

"Actually, I did have a chance to skim one of the files already on my desk. The defendant's name is Larkin. He's been charged with aggravated assault and battery, but the facts support, at most, a charge of exhibitionism or public nuisance."

I briefly outlined the facts for him.

Rantwist settled back in his chair and frowned. "There's something you need to understand about me and my administration, Kate. I have made it a goal of this office to rid this county of all sin, and especially sins of a sexual nature."

Rantwist spoke as if addressing a room full of constituents.

"I ran on a family values platform, and by electing me, the voters and God have spoken."

He thinks God voted for him?

"Larkin and people like him are deviants; agents of the devil, if you will. I will not allow Phoenix to become a present-day Sodom and Gomorrah. Under my administration, all evildoers will feel the full force of the law."

I was unaware of this side of Rantwist and was pretty sure the voting public was equally unaware. I'd done my homework before accepting the offer of employment at the county attorney's office. While it was true that Rantwist ran on a platform of family values, there was nothing in his campaign rhetoric to indicate the extent of his religious fervor, much less his divine appointment.

I turned around to see how Alan was handling this. He was nodding his head vigorously in agreement with Rantwist. I half expected him to genuflect. His eyes glowed, and he looked almost joyful, although it was kind of a manic, fevered joy. Alan showing any emotion was rare. Alan evidencing any form of joy or happiness was, according to office legend, unheard of. Clearly Alan was not going to provide a sane counterbalance to Rantwist's extremism. The two of them were riding on the Disoriented Express together.

I turned back to Rantwist and tried to reason with him, but in the pit of my stomach I knew that reason was irrelevant to this particular discussion.

"Larkin is being charged with a felony for which there is no factual or statutory basis. Your, um … cause won't be furthered if the charges are thrown out of court."

Rantwist went back to grinning.

"Here's how it works: The public defender's office is so overloaded, this case won't get before a judge on a motion to dismiss. Larkin is so dumb he won't know the difference. We offer Larkin a plea agreement with barely lowered charges and his over-worked, underpaid, half-brained attorney will recommend that he take the deal. Because the court system is overburdened, and judges are more interested in getting cases off their dockets than in whether a case is overcharged, no judge is going to question the plea. God's law will prevail over the ineffective statutes enacted by men."

Sadly, Rantwist's description of the legal system and prognosis of the likely outcome of Larkin's case were consistent with the situation in most large cities. I had some serious issues with the God's law thing, though.

"Where exactly did you find God's law about charging an exhibitionist, who has no prior record, with felony assault and battery?" I couldn't stop myself. It just came out.

There I was, being rational again.

Surprisingly, Rantwist did not take offense. "While the Scriptures provide us with direction, they do not provide us with details. God discloses the details to me through prayer."

I wondered whether he meant he prayed to God or it was the other way around.

I had never been big on religious fanatics. Over the years I'd learned that people who broadcast their religiosity were often the biggest crooks or bigots, using their religious convictions to rationalize dishonest or cruel behavior.

What the heck; since my relationship with Rantwist was already heading toward a cliff, I might as well step on the gas and go out *Thelma and Louise* style.

"What if God tells *me* something different?" I challenged.

This seemed to take Rantwist by surprise. He had not thought of the possibility that God might communicate with someone besides him. He regrouped quickly, though, and addressed me in condescending tones.

"Many think they are close to God, but my relationship with God is real, not imagined."

In other words, I was a nut, but he was a bigger nut.

I was clearly not going to convince Rantwist of anything other than what God told him or vice versa.

Rantwist stood and reached out to shake my hand in obvious dismissal. I was thrilled to take the hint.

I shook his hand and politely declined his offer to escort me to the elevator.

As soon as I was outside, I bolted for the elevator. Alan slithered out of Rantwist's office a few seconds behind me, but, thankfully, the elevator doors were open when I got there. I feigned an attempt to keep them open. I pounded the "close door" button. I shrugged apologetically as the doors slid closed before Alan could get in.

During the ride down I tried to let things sink in a bit. The side of Rantwist to which I had just been exposed came as a complete surprise. I could, I knew, work around Rantwist. I had done it often enough when I first started out as a young associate in a large law firm. I remembered one especially difficult partner who required preapproval of all client contacts initiated by an associate. I never had to contact any clients, though, because they all called *me*; after, of course, my secretary left them a message. Technical compliance is a powerful tool when you're bent on insubordination.

The issue now was whether I had the energy or the inclination to play those kinds of games at this stage in my career.

Chapter Two

I stopped at my office to get my purse and, after checking the hallway to make sure Alan wasn't lurking nearby, took the stairs to the underground parking lot.

The un-air-conditioned garage was stifling and smelled of trapped auto fumes. That probably explains why the lot is reserved for attorneys. Nobody likes attorneys. The temperature outside was in the hundreds, but at least the air quality was a step up.

The summers were the biggest negative I considered before I made my decision to move to Phoenix. At least they *were* the biggest negative before Rantwist shared his messianic delusions with me.

The hundred-plus degree weather started in late May and continued unabated until the end of September, when the temperature plunged into the nineties. The "temperate climate" travel brochures bragged about did not kick in until the end of October. The local chamber of commerce's official line is that it is a "dry heat," and that somehow makes it bearable. The citizens of Phoenix know better: when the thermometer hits a hundred and fifteen degrees, it's miserable, no matter how you try to qualify it.

I started my car, a silver Honda hybrid I purchased after I moved to Phoenix as part of my trimmed down lifestyle plan. The car I'd owned in Chicago was a Porsche Carrera 4S. I sanctimoniously figured that, having purchased the Honda, my duty to the environment was fulfilled.

Traffic outside was not heavy, which is another benefit of waiting until later to leave. Most of the buildings in the area housed government offices, and the 5:00 PM escape strategy was fairly universal.

It was still light out, and, according to the car's indicator, the temperature outside was a hundred and two. This was another fact the chamber of commerce had left out of their brochures: the days are longer in the summer when the temperatures are high and you don't want to be outside, but in the winter when the temperatures are in the seventies and eighties and the outdoors beckon, the days are ridiculously short. The typical workday in Phoenix for most people is eight to five. That means that in the winter you drive to work in the dark and come home in the dark, so all that good weather is unusable.

I desperately wanted to go to a nice restaurant, have a couple of drinks and a good dinner, and relax. First, though, I needed to get back to my condo and walk Ralph before he exploded. Ralph was used to being outside all day, and I'd had a difficult time introducing him to the idea of scheduled eliminations. His current compliance was based solely upon his trust in a consistent schedule. My failure to comply with that schedule could result in Ralph having a really nasty accident.

Admittedly, a high-rise condominium was not the best place for a dog as large as Ralph. But except for the aforementioned bowel and bladder control issues, he seemed to have settled in rather quickly, due above all to an excellent meal plan. At the dude ranch, Ralph was sporadically fed leftovers and was otherwise neglected, if not abused. He now enjoyed an overabundance of gourmet foods, thanks to my attempt to overcompensate for his past deprivation.

I parked in the underground garage of my building, took the elevator to the tenth floor, and raced to my condo. Checking my watch, I expected the worst as I opened the door.

Amazingly, Ralph had held it. He made it clear, though, that I was just in the nick of time. He rushed to the door without greeting me, grabbed his leash in his mouth from the coat rack in the hallway, and made for the elevator with me trailing behind. I attached the leash to his collar during the elevator ride, since he had not yet figured out how to do that for himself.

The part of town in which my building is located has few green areas, so Ralph had to forgo the benefits of a soft, grassy toilet seat and settle for pavement. Before I was able to push him toward the building's shadow into a venue less visible to the public, he squirted out a gallon or so of urine, then squatted and squeezed out an impressive mound of poop.

I didn't bother to clean up after him because his pile would dry up in the summer heat and blow away before morning. It sounded like a pretty nifty system until you realized that every time the wind came up, there was a good chance you were breathing dog turd particles.

On our return trip we ran into my next-door neighbor, Macy Gendler. We joined Macy in waiting for the elevator

Macy was a retired realtor from Brooklyn. She told me once how she got her unusual first name. It seems the immigration officers at Ellis Island asked her father to spell Yetta, which was her given name, but were unable to understand his thick accent. Finally, in frustration, he pointed to an advertisement for Macy's Department Store, figuring any name would do if it got them through immigration. So Yetta became Macy.

"God, it's hot," she said. "I'm *schvitzing* like crazy."

She patted Ralph on the head, and then craned her neck to look up at me. The top of Macy's head barely reached my shoulder when she stood straight. Ralph looked like a horse next to her.

"Did the nice doggy make?" she inquired politely.

"He did indeed. Phoenix has a new mountain," I answered.

"No matter. It'll be dust by tomorrow. How's work going?"

"So far, so good," I lied. "By the way, you lived in Phoenix when Stan Rantwist ran for county attorney, didn't you?"

"Sure. I saw him on television a couple of times. I don't follow politics here like I did in Brooklyn, but his campaign ads used to pop up between my two favorite TV shows—*Law and Order: Special Victims Unit* and *Law and Order: Criminal Intent*."

Good ad placement.

"Do you remember what his platform was?"

"The usual family values garbage, whatever the hell that is. I mean the family in the house next to us when I was growing up made a good living off of pot and magic mushrooms they grew in their basement. Illegal drug sales fit into their family values just fine. My uncle Al ran a prostitution ring out of his house. The ladies were nice, real classy. A lot of them had their kids living in the house with them. I guess you could say prostitution was part of their family values."

The elevator arrived, the three of us got in, and I punched the button for the tenth floor.

"Did Rantwist mention anything during his campaign about where his political ideas were coming from?"

Macy looked at me with a confused expression. "You mean like from the Republican Party or the Democratic Party? The guy's a Republican, right?"

"No, not like that. I mean more like ... like an other-world source."

"You mean like Martians?" she asked, still looking confused.

"No. Think white robes instead of green antennae."

"Oh, crap. The guy's a religious freak," said Macy in dismay.

I nodded sadly.

"Is it at least a deity I've heard of?" she asked.

"Yup. It appears he shares an office with none other than God Almighty, or maybe he allows God to sublet space. I'm not clear on the arrangements.

I thought I did my homework before accepting a job in Rantwist's office. I mean I knew the guy was conservative leaning, but I didn't pick up that his mission was god-directed. You're sure nothing like that came out in his campaign?"

Macy thought for a moment. "No, I didn't get anything like that from his ads, and I didn't see anything about it in the newspaper coverage of his campaign, either. A story like that woulda made headlines, right?

"Or maybe not," she corrected herself. "Sure, it would make headlines in Brooklyn, but maybe not in Arizona. The politics here are different. A friend from Temple told me one of the city councilmen wears a big pin that says, 'God Is on My Side.' I never figured God to show his hand like that."

We had reached our floor and were now standing in the hallway. Macy asked me if I wanted to come inside her condo and continue the discussion over drinks and munchies, but I begged off. It was getting late, and I needed serious food.

"Good luck with the boss," Macy said. She clucked sympathetically and patted my arm before we parted company.

Once inside my condo I had second thoughts about turning down Macy's invitation. I needed to be around people. Specifically, I needed to be around people who would agree with me that Rantwist was a nut and would help me figure out how the heck to handle it.

I punched my friend Joyce's number into the phone. Joyce and I first met in law school, and we renewed our friendship after running into each other at a bar convention some years ago. Joyce was a partner in a Phoenix law firm, and she was the first person I called when debating whether to move here.

She answered on the second ring. I could hear her son and husband arguing loudly in the background.

"Hi. It's Kate. I know this is late notice, but could you meet me at DeRoy's for dinner in about a half hour?"

"Yes, I would meet you in Baghdad if it meant getting out of this madhouse. Jeff can watch Geoffrey for a while. He can question the kid's parentage all he wants, but he is in fact Geoffrey's father and needs to take *some* responsibility for him. See you in a few."

Telephone conversations with Joyce were never long. She was the queen of time management.

I pulled into the parking lot of DeRoy's exactly thirty minutes later. Joyce was already there. I saw her red Corvette parked in the back of the lot. She'd parked it diagonally, taking up two spaces. The Corvette was her prize possession, and she insisted on parking it only where an adequate buffer zone between it and adjoining cars could be established. Sometimes this required that she park quite a distance from her destination. I once jokingly advised her to keep a smaller, more dispensable car in tow to commute to her Corvette—kind of like the way a dinghy works with a yacht.

I searched the room for Joyce among the restaurant's patrons as the door to DeRoy's closed behind me. DeRoy's was politically incorrect as far as restaurants go. It was smoke filled (despite the city's antismoking ordinance) and poorly lit. The walls were paneled with dark fake wood, the tabletops were gray Formica, and the seats were upholstered in red plastic. Electrical tape held the upholstery together in places where it had worn through or cracked. There wasn't a live plant or silk blossom in sight. The flower sprays on the tables were sorry specimens of the plastic genre. Various patrons, using matches or cigarettes, had experimented with the melting temperature of the plastic, which gave the plants a Daliesque quality.

The restaurant was packed. It was always packed.

Through the smoky haze I spotted Joyce waving from a back booth. I smiled and headed toward her, weaving my way carefully through tables and ducking the broad hand gestures made by patrons engrossed in conversation. The fact that cigarettes dangled from the fingers of several of those gesturing hands added an element of risk and adventure.

I negotiated the gauntlet without injury and plopped down in the seat opposite Joyce.

"So what's up?" she asked.

"A more appropriate inquiry would be 'What's down,' and the response would be 'Me,'" I answered glumly.

"I take it you had a rough day at work?"

"Is my life so lacking in depth and complexity that you immediately assume my job is the cause of my depression instead of, for example, a romantic liaison, predestined to fail due to a tragic flaw—in *him*, naturally?" I asked with a pained expression.

Joyce laughed raucously. One of the best things about Joyce was her laugh. There was nothing ladylike about it. It was loud, uninhibited, and thoroughly contagious.

I joined Joyce in a spate of giggling and snorting. Several people turned to stare at us, no doubt wondering if the Heimlich maneuver should be applied to one or both of us.

By the time a waitress came to take our order, we had managed to exert the level of control necessary to communicate with outsiders.

All of the waitresses at DeRoy's wear short black dresses, originally intended, no doubt, to be sexy. However, the typical DeRoy's waitress is over fifty, overweight (black is not slimming beyond a certain point), and surly. The footwear of choice is white, thick rubber-soled Rockports. Our waitress fit the DeRoy's mold perfectly, except she had added to her ensemble a dirty white cardigan from which sagged a button that read, "Obviously you have mistaken me for someone who gives a shit."

"Whaddaya want?" she asked brusquely, flipping through her order pad looking for a clean page.

I doubted she would find one.

We ordered wine and then plunged into more controversial territory.

"What's the special today?" Joyce asked sweetly.

Our waitress sighed the sigh of the oppressed.

"S'written up front on the blackboard. You know; the one you can't miss when you walk in?"

Joyce was not intimidated

"I guess I must have missed it. Can you tell me what it says?"

"It don't *say* nothin'. Ya gotta read it."

"Come on! At least give me a suggestion," persisted Joyce.

"Okay. You need to get your roots retouched."

It was a standoff.

Joyce capitulated and ordered a hamburger with fries. I ordered the same.

The waitress grunted and left, presumably, but not necessarily, to take our order to the kitchen.

Another waitress appeared shortly with our wine, which was served in a carafe that looked suspiciously like an old mayonnaise jar. She produced two juice glasses from her apron pockets and plunked them down in front of us.

"Why do we keep coming here?" I asked.

"You come here because of a deep-seated need for abuse in all areas of your life. I come here because *you* like it," said Joyce.

"Thank you, Dr. Joyce." I poured the wine, picked out the stuff floating on top, and handed her a glass.

I raised my own. "To us," I said, and we clicked our drinks together. "So why don't you update me on your life before we get into the much lengthier discussion of mine?"

Joyce smiled, and proceeded to regale me with stories about her precocious little boy, Geoffrey.

Geoffrey surpassed his contemporaries in all areas of child development. At six years old he had a hefty vocabulary which incorporated the legal jargon of his lawyer mother and the medical jargon of his physician father. The latest Geoffrey anecdote involved him telling his elementary school teacher she was a schizophrenic, resulting in his banishment to the realm of time-out after his teacher looked up *schizophrenic* in the dictionary and realized she'd been insulted.

Geoffrey had not taken his punishment quietly. He had claimed violations of free speech and due process and had asserted the right to an appeal. The loud discussion I heard in the background when I called Joyce earlier was the result of a disagreement between father and son over the type of therapy to which his teacher should be forced to submit in order to address her obviously deviant behavior. Apparently Geoffrey favored a Freudian approach, while his father argued in favor of Skinnerian behavioral therapy.

Joyce showed me the latest photographs of her genius child. I made appreciative noises over snapshots of a serious little boy staring challengingly into the camera lens. His Big Bird T-shirt seemed at odds with his expression. A business suit would have been more appropriate.

After we exhausted the subject of Geoffrey, it was my turn. I told Joyce about my meetings with MJ, Sam, Alan, and Rantwist.

"It's not going to work," she said when I was through.

"What's not going to work?" I countered. "Rantwist's agenda? Alan's stalking and spying? Sam's obsession with Johnny Depp? MJ's fashion sense or, more appropriately, nonsense?"

"You. You working for Rantwist. You can try to work around him, but why? You're too old for that, and quite honestly, you suck at it. You've got this compulsion to say whatever is on your mind. That approach will not work with an egotistical and delusional authority figure like Rantwist."

"So what's the answer? Should I quit and let some suck-up replace me who does whatever Rantwist says? What good would that do? Rantwist needs to be restrained, not flattered."

"It would do *you* good, because you'd get out of an untenable situation and move on with your life. I sense, though, that the crusader element of your personality left over from your defense-attorney days is alive and well. You can't stand to see people railroaded by the system. Once a defense attorney, always a defense attorney."

I opened my mouth to argue, but then realized she was right. My practice in Chicago had been stressful and frustrating, but deep inside I'd always identified with the underdog. Sure, most of the defendants I represented were guilty of *something*. But they needed the help of someone like me to make sure they weren't steamrolled by the process and unjustly punished as the result of the overkill strategy universal among prosecutors. Which was, oh damn, exactly what Rantwist was trying to do, albeit with more egregious overreaching than your typical prosecutor.

I fell back in my seat. "Oh my God, you're right. I still see everything from the point of view of the defendant. I'm no good as a prosecutor. I can't blindly advocate for the State to impose excess charges and let the system handle the issue of innocence or guilt. The system doesn't work."

Joyce shook her head. "Sheesh. Don't be so hard on yourself. I didn't say you could never be a good prosecutor. What I'm saying is that you have an inborn sense of fairness. A sense of fairness, by the way, that *all* attorneys—heck, all *people*—should have. But Rantwist seems to lack this capacity in even the most elemental form, and if you stay at the county attorney's office, you will be at odds with him constantly. You'll be miserable."

Joyce had a good point; several of them, in fact. I realized I should follow her advice and quit, but my damned crusader's instinct overrode reason. Yessir. Find a hopeless situation, and count me in. Custer would have loved me. *Here, Kate, wear this target on your chest, don't carry any weapons, and then go stand on that mound over there and yell, "Cowboys rule."*

"I think I need to give it a chance at the county attorney's office. I can at least try to introduce an element of reason to Rantwist's quest. I can't believe I'm the only one who doesn't go along with his wacko philosophy. There have to be others who feel the same way I do."

Joyce sighed. "So what if there are? As long as Rantwist's still in charge the only thing you will have done is find some buddies to stand around the water cooler with and bitch. If you're going to be a glutton for punishment and stay in the county attorney's office, instead of putting yourself through hell for the next four years, or more if the guy is reelected, why don't you 'out' Rantwist and let public opinion handle the rest before things get too weird?"

"I would, but right now it's his word against mine. I doubt Alan will corroborate anything I say about our meeting with Rantwist. The guy is a remora. I need more evidence. I need witnesses to Rantwist's conduct who will back me up."

Joyce took a sip of wine. "Here's another possibility. Maybe there's really nothing to worry about. Maybe Rantwist's walk is not as nutty as his talk. I mean, you haven't actually seen him apply his god-directed theory of crime and punishment, right? So far, except for one offbeat charge, it's just talk; weird talk, but still only talk. Maybe tomorrow it will turn out it was all a joke, and the overcharged file you got was only a test to see if you are paying attention and doing your job."

We looked at each other and both said, "Nah."

CHAPTER THREE

I didn't get much sleep that night, but it had less to do with my concerns about Rantwist than with Ralph's sleep cycle, which consisted of snore, chase imaginary rabbits, fart, and repeat. Since Ralph slept in bed with me, it was tough to ignore him. I'd tried to get him to sleep elsewhere. I even bought him a huge, soft, fluffy doggy bed with his name embroidered on it. I now used the doggy bed as a floor cushion.

I rolled out of bed at six o'clock and took Ralph out for his morning dump. He was more selective than usual, sniffing every inch of pavement and every potted plant, mailbox, and hydrant before making his choice, which turned out to be the same place he went the night before. I guess there's nothing better than that home-cooked smell.

Cal Jenkins, the occupant of a second-floor condo, was coming out of the elevator when Ralph and I came back. Cal was ex-FBI and, at 79, still looked as if he could take on a criminal or two. Macy had the hots for him.

Today he was wearing jogging shorts and a tight T-shirt. He held the elevator for us.

"Hey, thanks, Cal." I said. "You heading out to do some jogging?"

"I prefer to think of it as a neighborhood patrol using jogging as my cover," he replied.

I thought, *He really needs a hobby.*

"How is your job at the county attorney's office going?"

"Fine," I lied.

"Glad to hear it. Say, your neighbor Macy told me you used to be on the defense side. Maybe we can meet for coffee sometime, and I can give you a few tips about the prosecutor gig."

"Love to," I called out as the elevator doors closed. Macy would be so jealous.

I grabbed the newspaper off the floor of the entry as I ushered Ralph into our condo. Once unleashed, he immediately charged over to the breakfast table and jumped up on a chair.

I had turned the coffeemaker on before our walk, so the coffee was ready and waiting. I poured myself a cup and set a bowl of water in front of Ralph. Once seated, I opened the local section of the newspaper and handed Ralph the ads. He liked to look at the pictures.

On the front page was an article about the robbery of a nearby convenience store. Convenience store robberies had become so common, not only in Phoenix but all over the country, that I wondered why the newspaper bothered to cover this one, much less put it on the front page. Now if Phoenix had gone a day *without* a convenience store robbery, that would be front page news. I read the article out of habit, since many of my former clients had been, and probably still were, in the convenience store robbing business.

It turned out this was not a run-of-the-mill robbery. The crime, which was recorded by the store's surveillance cameras, was committed by a female about six feet tall with shoulder-length blond hair. She was wearing six-inch heels (the paper did not say whether the six feet tall estimate included the heels), a pink linen suit, and sunglasses. According to the article, the cameras showed the robber waving a nail file at the cashier, a short Hispanic woman, who responded by handing over the money from the cash register.

When asked later why she so readily handed the money over when the only weapon in sight was a nail file, the cashier responded, "Why not?"

The article dubbed the robber the "Paris Hilton Bandit" and notified the public that she was still at large, though she no doubt had changed clothes: six-inch heels are real killers. The public was advised to report anyone acting suspiciously to the police.

The police were going to get a lot of calls. What constitutes suspicious behavior is largely a subjective determination. They should have been more specific, maybe even provided a checklist.

I glanced at the clock. It was getting late. I needed to dress for work pronto. I shoved a handful of Trix in my mouth and put dog food in Ralph's dish. I sprinkled some Trix on top so he wouldn't feel deprived. A half hour later I was stumbling to the elevator, wearing one shoe and struggling to get the other shoe on before the elevator came. Macy stuck her head out her door and yelled, "You gonna still work for the nut?"

I said I was, but told her not to worry, since I had lots of practice dealing with nuts.

"Phooey," she said.

In the garage I noticed that Cal had parked his monster SUV next to my car. I sucked my stomach in and sidestepped through the narrow gap. As I was squeezing through the even narrower gap between my opened car door and the front seat, I happened to glance into Cal's truck. A blond wig lay on the front seat.

The wig was probably used for dress up by one of Cal's many granddaughters, whose toys and spare clothes littered the backseat of the SUV. He was constantly picking up or dropping off one or more of his granddaughters at the hysterical behest of his daughter, who worked at a utility company and, with three daughters and no husband, often needed her dad's help, and probably the help of a good analyst.

Traffic on the way to the office was bumper to bumper, which was typical. The woman in the car in front of me was applying her makeup, and the man in the car behind me appeared to be trimming his nose hairs. The general lack of driver concentration combined with the stop-and-go traffic made for a slow yet challenging commute.

I was running late, so by the time I pulled into the garage, nearly every space was filled. I ended up parking on the roof lot, which meant the interior of my car would reach a hundred and twenty degrees plus by the end of the day. The temperature outside was already in the nineties, and it was only a little past nine o'clock.

MJ was waiting for me when I reached my office. She'd made herself comfortable in my chair.

"Good morning, MJ. Get out of my chair," I said.

MJ complied but took her time. Today she was wearing a red T-shirt that said "bite me," a pair of black leggings, and red heels.

"What, no new tattoos? No new piercings?" I asked.

"I got a new piercing. You just can't see it. Do you want me to take off my pants and show it to you?"

I shuddered. "Please don't. So did you finish the case summaries?"

MJ waved her hand at the stack of files on my desk. "Yes, ma'am. Each case summary is attached to the front of the corresponding case file."

I was dumbstruck. I had not expected this. Based on my past experience with MJ types, I had predicted at least a week's worth of procrastination accompanied by excuses of great length and originality. I was almost disappointed. I'd been looking forward to an especially creative performance by MJ. Also, now I had no reason not to go over the files.

"Anything interesting?" I asked once I had recovered enough to speak.

"Same ol' same ol'. Except the new boss seems to be a bit harsh on certain types of crimes. I've never seen a charge of felony two for prostitution with no priors. It'd be one thing if she shot the undercover cop after he showed his badge or something. But there was nothin' like that. There's also a felony charge against some guy busted for whacking off in a porn shop booth. Hell, why do they have booths in porn shops if they're not for whacking off?"

I shrugged. "Ya got me. Out of curiosity, have you been hearing the same kind of thing from the other paralegals? Is everyone getting cases like this?"

"Seems that way. Rhoda, Dan Siever's paralegal, said they got one with a felony charge for adultery."

I made a mental note to talk to Dan Siever.

"You gonna need anything else today? 'Cuz my crotch hurts like a bitch, and I'm thinking of taking the rest of the day off."

"By all means … take the rest of the day off, but never, ever mention your crotch problems to me again," I said, grimacing.

"Hey, I can't help it if I'm an honest person. I tell it like it is, and the way it is, is it hurts and the ring keeps snagging on my panties."

"Go."

"Fine. See you tomorrow. Maybe."

As MJ left, I noticed her gait was unnaturally bowlegged and slow.

I picked up the employee directory on my desk and looked up Dan Siever. His office was on the second floor. Dan too was part of the major felony division, but I had not met him yet.

I was halfway out the door when I noticed that Alan was in my office. I had no idea how long he'd been there. As usual, his entry was noiseless, and, moreover, in his brown suit (the same one he'd worn the day before), he blended into the furniture fairly well.

He was sitting in the sagging chair and scratching away at a white stain on his lapel. His attempt to remove the stain only seemed to make it worse.

"Alan? Did you need something?"

He looked up from his lapel, but continued to scratch at it with a fingernail.

"Cream," he said.

I gathered this was not a response to my question, but was in reference to the source of the stain.

I waited.

He quit scratching. "The County Attorney asked that I speak to you. He is concerned that you may have misunderstood what he said last night."

Thank God, I thought. *Maybe Rantwist accidentally ingested a hallucinatory drug before we got to his office and didn't mean any of the God stuff.*

I returned to my desk and sat down. "Go on," I said.

"Wait. Let me close your door so we can have some privacy."

Closing my door would in no way insure privacy, but I resisted pointing it out.

The door-closing ceremony concluded, Alan sat down and leaned forward confidentially.

He said something, but as was the case yesterday, I couldn't make out what he was saying.

"Alan, I can't hear you. Could you speak up a bit?"

Alan made no attempt to increase his volume but leaned closer to me instead. His halitosis just about knocked me out.

"The County Attorney wants me to underline the fact that this is his administration, and if you are not one hundred percent willing to assist in attaining the goals of his administration, you should look for employment elsewhere. No hard feelings."

I fought the urge to quit on the spot and give Alan a hard feeling right to the nose. I reasoned with the angry part of myself that if I was going to keep my job long enough to "out" Rantwist, I needed to appear to be a good and loyal soldier.

I smiled brightly. "I understand the county attorney's position, Alan, and rest assured that I back the county attorney one hundred percent."

Alan smiled and patted my shoulder, letting his hand linger longer than what I considered socially acceptable.

"Well, then," he said, smiling, "I'm glad we are in agreement."

"I think we should pray now," I said reverently. I figured if I was going to pretend to go along, I might as well play it to the hilt.

Alan looked surprised, then pleased. He placed his clammy, dried-cream-particle-covered hand over mine and bowed his head. A sprinkling of dandruff landed on my desktop.

"Dear Lord," I said, "please bless the county attorney and his mission, and help me to be his good servant." I was sure God wouldn't object to my little lie. He knew it was for a good cause.

Alan squeezed my hand.

"Maybe we could meet for a cocktail sometime," he said.

I gave him my best wide-eyed look of innocence. Admittedly, I was a little rusty at that kind of thing. "Oh, Alan, I don't partake of spirits," I said with what I hoped was the proper touch of self-righteousness.

Alan looked nonplussed. He tried again. "Well, maybe we can meet for coffee."

"Caffeine is a drug," I said.

"We'll make it decaf, then."

I couldn't think of a good objection to decaf.

"Decaf it is. I'll give you a call," he said, giving me a wink and a yellow-toothed grin.

Alan gave my hand a parting squeeze before sidling out of the room.

Man, did I need a drink.

I headed for Dan Siever's office again. En route I stopped in the employee lounge and filled my mug with coffee; black, no sugar. The hard stuff.

Dan's door was closed, so, trying to set an example for the staff, I knocked.

There was a long silence, and then a voice said uncertainly, "Come in?"

I walked in, extended my hand, and introduced myself.

Dan was a thin, gaunt, gray-haired man. His skin was "prison-white," so called because it was the color of a prisoner's skin after he hadn't seen the light of day for a few years. I guessed he was on the tall side, but it was hard to tell because he did not bother to stand when I entered. He wore a navy pinstriped suit with a red tie, which was definitely a step up from Alan's haberdashery.

"I'm sorry to take so long answering the door. It's just that nobody around here knocks, and I didn't know what to think. It took me a while to even identify what the sound was.

"I'm Dan Siever, by the way. Glad to meet you. I saw your name in a memo this morning. You just joined our division, right? You're from Chicago?"

"Yes to both questions. I really haven't had a chance to get my teeth into any cases yet, though. I've only been here a couple of weeks, and so far everything's pled out," I said.

"Please take a seat. My manners are really lacking. You've been here two weeks already? I'm sorry I haven't come by to introduce myself and welcome you aboard. I swear though, I only got the memo this morning."

He shuffled through the mess of papers on his desk, pulled out a pink paper (it would be pink), and triumphantly held it out to me. "See?"

I took the memo from him and noticed it was dated two weeks ago. Either the interoffice mail was extremely slow, or Dan was extremely disorganized. By the looks of his desk, I'd put my money on the latter.

I smiled and handed the memo back to him and sat down in a chair nearly identical to the one in my office, except this one was in slightly better shape. I guess seniority has its privileges.

"I just got a stack of new cases but really haven't had a good look at them yet. Can you give me an idea of what I'm in for? I know our division only deals with felonies, but do just a few types of crimes dominate, or are they all over the map?"

Dan tented his hands and rested his chin on his fingertips. He looked like he was about to give a closing argument.

"As you probably already know, the major felony division only handles first and second degree felonies. That usually means stuff like murder, aggravated robbery, rape, and the larger drug busts."

"Usually?" I asked with feigned innocence.

"Yeah. The new administration has thrown a few unusual cases into the mix. For instance, I'm handling a felony adultery case. I'm not even sure we have the authority to charge adultery as a felony. According to the statutes, the most you can charge for adultery is a class three misdemeanor. I checked with the charging division, though, and they said the decision came right from the top."

"Are you going ahead with the prosecution?"

He shrugged. "Sure."

"Maybe you should talk to Rantwist about it."

Dan snickered. "You've never worked for the government before, have you?"

I shook my head no.

"Well, let me explain how it works. Believe me, I know. Rantwist is the third county attorney I've worked for. They come and they go, and some are easier to work with than others. The trick to keeping your job is to follow orders and keep a low profile. They can't fire you if they don't know your name."

I persisted. "But the defendants are represented by counsel. Won't they raise a stink? I mean, even an attorney fresh out of law school knows enough to ask for dismissal of charges that aren't authorized by statute."

Dan grinned. "This is the fun part. The public defender's office here is so overworked, stretched so thin, that unless it's a capital punishment case, they'll plead it out to any lesser charge you offer. Take a closer look at your files. I bet most, if not all, of the defendants are represented by court appointed public defenders."

I'd heard nearly identical reasoning from Rantwist.

"So how many cases actually go to trial, then?" I asked.

"Very few. Most just plead out and slide quietly through the system. In the last year I've had two cases go to trial. Both involved defendants with enough money to hire private counsel. Fortunately, that doesn't happen too often. All in all, this is a pretty easy gig. Like I said, though, you have to keep a low profile."

My dismay must have shown on my face.

"This must be a lot different from Chicago. What'd you do up there?"

"After law school I worked for a large firm doing civil trial work for a couple of years. Then I went into partnership with another attorney. We specialized in criminal defense."

Dan laughed uproariously at this bit of news. "Well, welcome to the other side. Don't worry. You'll get used to it. Just remember what I said: follow orders and keep your head down."

I forced a light laugh that came out more like a croak. I was pretty disgusted by Dan's attitude, but was trying not to show it. Back in my Chicago days I would have splayed someone like Dan Siever the same way Mel Gibson was in the last scene of *Braveheart*.

"I guess I'd better be going," I said, standing. "I have a load of case summaries to read. Thanks so much for your time and your advice."

Dan looked surprised. "Case summaries? You did case summaries? You *are* diligent."

"Actually, MJ, my paralegal, did them."

I left before he could comment.

CHAPTER FOUR

I stopped off at the employee lounge on my way back to my office. As I was refilling my coffee mug, I heard Alan's voice behind me.

"I thought you didn't like caffeine," he murmured in his annoying half whisper.

"Who told you that?" I said.

"You did."

"When?"

"This morning when I was in your office."

"I don't remember you being in my office."

"But … it was just this morning."

"You must have imagined it."

Thankfully, Alan did not follow me to my office. He was probably still trying to figure out which one of us was losing his or her mind.

I started reading the case summaries prepared by MJ. They were really quite good. I checked the files on a couple of them and found that she had zeroed in on the pertinent facts, strengths, and weaknesses of the cases. Under all that iridescent red hair was a good brain. Who would have guessed?

There were twenty-five cases in all, and of these, six were overcharged. Each of the six involved a minor sex crime. Something else struck me as odd about my caseload. None of the files involved drug-related crimes. In Chicago, drug crimes made up at least ninety percent of the criminal court docket. It was possible that the drug cases were being handled by a special division, but then I remembered that Dan included "large drug busts" in the list of crimes handled by the our division. I completely dismissed the possibility that Phoenix was a drug-free city. Anyone who believed that would have to be, well, on drugs.

I finished reading the file summaries and was busy writing on a legal pad, prioritizing my caseload, when Sam knocked and walked in. He was wearing a spectacular black Armani suit with a pink shirt and darker pink tie. I couldn't be sure, but it looked like he was wearing just the tiniest bit of eyeliner. He had to be either very confident of his masculinity or gay. Of course he could be both. Whatever the case, I thought the eyeliner really made his eyes pop and thought I might try some myself.

He stopped in front of my desk and looked at me pointedly. I figured me having to start the discussion was going to be a standard practice. "You wanted something, Sam?"

Sam performed his brushing-off-the-chair ritual before sitting down and, once seated, followed up with the non-existent lint removal routine. "I assume you have had time to review your files. That being the case, I am here to discuss my assignments."

A mote of dust, lit by the sunlight coming through my window, floated toward Sam. I stared in fascination as he watched the slow, erratic flight of the particle with something akin to horror on his face. He flapped his hand furiously, apparently trying to create enough of a breeze to blow it in the other direction. The particle wafted toward the window. Disaster had been averted.

"Look, I'm not crazy," he said.

Apparently I didn't look convinced, and I wasn't.

"It takes too long to explain, but trust me; the air in Phoenix is full of dogshit particles."

And I knew why.

I steered the conversation back to business. "I have reviewed the files superficially, and I'm in the process of prioritizing them. I should have your assignments tomorrow. I will call you when they're ready."

Sam nodded curtly with clenched jaw like a soldier receiving his first battle order and started to rise.

A question occurred to me. Sam, so far as I knew, had been employed by the county attorney's office for several years, yet his attitude seemed to be fairly gung ho. Why? On impulse, I asked him, "Why the enthusiastic attitude? I mean, it's great, but you're not exactly in step with the mainstream here."

Sam hesitated. His eyes reflected uncertainty. I could tell he was deciding whether to trust me.

Apparently, and inexplicably from my point of view, trust seemed to win out. He sat down again.

"I realize personal biases have no place in the office, but I am concerned with the direction some of our cases are taking. You see, I'm gay," he said.

I wasn't expecting this. Certainly I had a suspicion he might be gay. I just wasn't expecting an announcement. Moreover, I was unclear as to what his gay status had to do with his work ethic.

I nodded. "Okay, so you're gay. Which cases are bothering you?"

He let out a long breath. "Thank goodness you don't have a problem with the gay thing. It's probably because you're from Chicago. Being gay is probably no big deal in Chicago. You've got to understand, though: in Phoenix, it's different. There's a conservative element here that would enjoy seeing people like me strung up in the public square."

"Don't kid yourself. We've got 'em like that in Chicago, too," I said with a grimace.

"But here it's … well, it's more institutionalized. At least it is after the last election."

"What do you mean?"

Sam stood and quickly moved to the door. After peering down the outside corridor in each direction, he eased it shut. He reached into his pocket and pulled out a small brown rubber wedge which he then shoved under the door.

My excitement knew no bounds. "What an amazing little device. What's it called? Where can I get one?"

"It's a doorstop, and you can get one at any hardware store," he said curtly. "Can we get back to our discussion now?

Sam seemed annoyed that I'd shown more interest in the doorstop than I did in his big announcement.

I made a mental note to buy one of those wonderful gadgets as soon as possible. Sam had retaken his seat and was jealously glaring at the doorstop, which he apparently viewed as competition for my attention. I knew he was upset because he had not bothered to brush off the seat of his chair before sitting down.

I cleared my throat.

Sam looked at me and reassured himself that he had my full focus. "Ralphy McDonald, another investigator in our division …"

"Ralphy?" I interrupted. "What kind of mother would name her child Ralphy?" Or her dog, for that matter.

"Yes, Ralphy," Sam said impatiently. "She's a woman."

Of course. "Sorry I interrupted," and I really was.

"So Ralphy tells me Randy Fulbrick, the deputy county attorney she is assigned to, has five cases where the defendants are charged with felony sodomy. In the past, the sodomy statutes were used to go after gays, but they haven't been enforced for years. We've never handled a sodomy charge, much less a felony sodomy charge, during the six years I've worked here."

I flipped open a copy of the criminal law statutes lying on my desk.

"The statutes say sodomy is a class three misdemeanor. So what's felony sodomy? Is that when an especially bad wardrobe choice is involved?"

That got a smile out of Sam.

"No, although even that would make more sense." He leaned over and rubbed a nonexistent smudge off one of his exquisite, expensive looking shoes. "The facts in each case allege nothing more than some canoodling between two consenting males. The point is, if you have any cases like that, I'd appreciate it if you could bring them to the attention of the county attorney."

"Why don't Randy or Ralphy bring their cases to the county attorney's attention?" I asked reasonably.

"Because Randy and Ralphy don't want to rock the boat."

"Well, I don't have any cases involving sodomy charges, but if I get one in the future, why don't *you* bring it to the county attorney's attention?"

"Because I report to you, and I don't want to go over your head."

"I would have no problem with you going over my head on a matter like this."

He pursed his lips and then blurted, "I can't. I need this job. Rantwist probably doesn't know I exist, and I want to keep it that way."

So you're not that different from everyone else around here after all, I thought.

"I don't even know why I came to you," Sam said, rushing his words. "Rantwist hired you. You're probably in on his antigay strategy. By the way, you're the only one in the office I've told that I'm gay, which was probably a *really* big mistake. Please don't 'out' me."

I was pretty sure everyone on the staff had already guessed.

I felt bad for him, though. He seemed to be in real distress. I had nothing against gays and was surprised the sodomy laws were still on the books in Arizona. Most states had abolished them for the very reason Sam had stated: their purpose was to target the gay community.

"Look, Sam, I'll let you in on a little secret. I've already talked to Rantwist, not specifically about sodomy charges—like I said, we don't have any files like that—but about another felony charge not authorized by statute. I got nowhere. It seems Rantwist is on a crusade to cleanse Phoenix of certain elements."

I told him about the felony assault charges against the exhibitionist, the five new files MJ just brought in, and the cases being handled by Siever.

He scowled. "Did Rantwist explain exactly why he's on this crusade? I mean, he ran for office on a conservative platform, but nothing like this. This is beyond conservative; it's reactionary. Actually, it's beyond reactionary, even; it's nuts."

"Rantwist said his orders come from above."

"You're kidding. You mean the attorney general or the governor?"

"Think higher."

Sam gasped. "The president?"

I shook my head. Sam looked puzzled. Gradually a look of understanding appeared on his face.

"He's a religious nut," he said flatly.

I nodded.

"Great. So now what do we do?" he moaned.

"What do you mean, 'we'?" I responded sarcastically. "You mean what am *I* going to do. You've already made it clear you won't do anything to rock the boat."

Sam had the good sense to look ashamed. "I'm sorry. You're right. I'm a wimp."

I glanced at the clock. It was already eleven forty-five. I I figured it was too close to noon to try to get any more work done before lunch.

"Sam, what do you say you and I track down MJ and have lunch together? Maybe we can figure something out."

"I'd love to go to lunch, but I'm not sure about MJ. I don't know if she's still in the office," he said. "I saw her this morning, and she said something about a bleeding hole in her nether regions. She said she might be going home early."

I punched MJ's extension number into the phone, trying hard not to think about her bleeding nether regions. I was surprised when she answered.

"You up for lunch?" I asked.

"You paying?" she asked.

"Yes."

"Then count me in. Meet you in the lobby."

CHAPTER FIVE

Sam excused himself to use the "little boys' room" and said he would meet me at the elevator. I visited the women's lounge and met him a few minutes later. We found MJ waiting by the front door in the lobby. As we left the building, a draft caught us from behind. We simultaneously exclaimed "My hair!" and scrambled to smooth, spike, or plump our respective coifs into place. Sam was the only one of us who had a mirror.

We reached a consensus on where to have lunch and headed for Casa de Paco, a Mexican restaurant two blocks away.

The outside heat was unbearable. We were dying of thirst by the time we got to the restaurant. Whoever Paco was, he understood Arizona in the summer, because a pitcher of cold water was waiting for us at the table where we were seated.

After a brief struggle over control of the water pitcher, which I won by playing the boss card, I poured myself a glass of water, then passed the pitcher to MJ. We all ordered cheese enchiladas, the specialty of the house. Within minutes our waitress emerged from the kitchen with three plates piled high with the cheesiest enchiladas I'd ever seen.

We dug in. I tried to start a conversation between mouthfuls, but it was rough talking through all the cheese. "Howurufullin', MJ?"

"Whuh?" she said, trying to eat her way through a long string of cheese suspended between her teeth and the plate.

I swallowed and tried again. "How are you feeling?"

"Guhl," she said. Then, after finishing the cheese string, added, "But the pain comes and goes. I may feel worse this afternoon and have to leave early."

We ate in silence for a while. Eventually I put my fork down, having done as much damage to the enchiladas as I could. I wiped the grease off my chin in response to Sam's request that I do so.

"MJ, Sam and I were talking this morning after you and I spoke."

"Were you talking about me?" she interrupted. "You were, weren't you? It's my pussy ring, isn't it? It bugs you." She was smirking like a naughty child.

"No, we were not talking about you." I didn't respond to the second part of her surmise. Her pussy ring did bug me. In fact it nauseated me to think about it.

I forged ahead. "We were talking about some of the cases in the office, and, in particular…"

Sam tensed and hissed "Shhhhhh. The weasel just walked in with Siever."

I didn't have to ask who the weasel was even though I had my back to the door and hadn't seen Alan and Dan come in.

Stupidly, I turned around to look. They spotted me. I smiled and gave a short wave, then turned back to MJ and Sam in a manner intended to politely acknowledge their presence but deter further communication.

I felt a tap on my shoulder.

Clearly, I needed to work on my nonverbal cues.

I turned slightly and looked up into Alan's face. He looked especially weasel-ish from this angle.

"Doing business over lunch?" he asked.

"Yes. It seems like this is the only time all of us can get together," I answered lightly.

Alan snorted through his nose. Sam stifled a high-pitched scream and ducked to dodge whatever real or imagined snot particles Alan had shot into the air.

"Well, don't forget to take a break once in a while. Remember, my offer of drinks after work—either alcoholic or nonalcoholic, your choice—is still open." He winked at me then nodded curtly to MJ and Sam—the latter of whom seemed to be looking for something under the table—and went back to his booth. I noticed Dan had already ordered a pitcher of margaritas. That should make for an interesting afternoon.

Our privacy having been invaded, I hurriedly paid the bill, and we left. The heat outside once again made civilized discussion impossible.

When we got to the lobby of our building, I told MJ and Sam that I really needed to get some work done, so we would have to continue our meeting another day. Since it was Friday, I asked them to come to my office at ten o'clock on Monday morning. Sam said he would be there. MJ said she would try to be there, but her health was iffy these days.

CHAPTER SIX

I spent the rest of the afternoon prioritizing my files, checking the docket, and working on responses to motions that were due. I skipped out at four thirty, afraid Alan might try to catch me for a drink if I hung around any longer.

Ralph was thrilled when I came home earlier than usual. He wasn't so thrilled with the frying-pan hot pavement at that hour. As we walked, he stuck to the shade when he could and whined when there was no shade to be had. I took pity on him and headed across the street to a café that had an outdoor patio with a misting system. Even with the misting system in full operation, offering the hope of respite from the heat, the patio was almost empty, so we had no trouble finding a table. Ralph flopped down next to me, and I ordered wine and a cold glass of water for me and a bowl of ice water for Ralph.

I chugged the wine and ordered another glass. Only social propriety prevented me from ordering a bottle of chardonnay with a straw. The first glass of wine hit me as the second glass arrived at my table, so I felt pretty relaxed, and life seemed slightly better.

The café was located in an upscale outdoor mall, so the people-watching opportunities were excellent. Even with temperatures in the hundreds, the siren call of Saks Fifth Avenue was strong, and there were a fair number of shoppers out, most of them women. I am a shoe-aholic and a purse-aholic, so I focused primarily on the women's footwear and handbags. I observed one well-dressed young lady carrying a Louis Vuitton bag in a style I had not seen and immediately wanted. Maybe I would wander over to Saks after my wine break and see what they had in stock. Fortunately, the mall was dog friendly. All the stores allowed dogs inside, provided they were on a leash and well trained. I glanced down at Ralph, who was asleep with his head resting on my foot. He was snoring, and a string of drool dangled from his mouth. At least he was on a leash. I could probably go in and complete whatever transactions I needed to before anyone figured out we were in violation of the "well trained" part of the rule.

I was sipping my wine delicately in an attempt to overcome the wine-guzzling initial impression I'd made on the waiter, when my eyes locked on to an exceptionally nice Ferragamo shoulder bag. A tap on my arm interrupted my mental calculations as to whether I could afford *both* purses.

"May I join you?"

It was Cal. "Certainly," I responded, gesturing to the empty chair next to me. He was still wearing the jogging shorts he'd had on earlier. "Don't tell me you've been out jogging all day."

He laughed. "Believe me, if I had, I'd be a lot sweatier than I am now. Actually, in this heat I'd probably be dead."

He must have seen me look at his shorts. "Don't worry. I've done two loads of wash since you saw me this morning. My clothes are relatively sweat free."

I groaned. "You just reminded me. I haven't done my laundry since I moved into my condo. I've really got to get it done this weekend."

"Oh, I can help you out. A working woman like you needs a break. You shouldn't be doing laundry on the weekend. When you get home, just put your stuff outside your door. I'll pick it up and take care of it when I take care of my stuff tomorrow."

"Really? Are you sure? I mean, you just did laundry today. I don't want you making a special trip just for me."

"I wash my clothes every day, so it's no problem at all."

Every day? This man needed to do something else with his life—but not until he finished my laundry.

"Okay. Offer accepted. Thank you very much."

Cal ordered a club soda and asked if I wanted anything more. I shook my head no. Two glasses of wine had been enough to bring about the desired buzz.

"So how is work going?" he asked. "Any interesting cases?"

He listened intently as I described a few of my files. I didn't mention the oddball misdemeanors-charged-as-felonies, but instead told him about a run-of-the-mill burglary and a murder I was handling. Cal's interest did not waver. He interrupted me only a few times, and when he did, he asked intelligent questions. I got the feeling he really missed the FBI, so I added a little more color to my case descriptions for his benefit.

"By the way, did you hear about the robbery here in the neighborhood?" I asked after I finished the color commentary on my cases.

Cal shook his head. "No."

"I'm surprised. It's been in the papers and on the television news."

"There's no television in the laundry room."

"Well, let me tell you: It was pretty interesting. It happened at the Mighty Mart and was all caught on the store's security camera. The robber was wearing six-inch high heels. Can you imagine? I can't make it two steps in six-inch heels."

"Were they able to make an identification?"

"No, but the robber was pretty unique looking. She had blond hair and excellent taste in clothes, but she was pretty big for a female. There can't be many women around of that size."

"Big as in fat, or big as in tall?" Cal's tone was oddly testy.

"Big as in tall," I said.

His face relaxed.

"And the weapon was a nail file, a dinky little nail file," I added.

Cal laughed. "Welcome to the wild, or perhaps more correctly, the odd West."

"I only hope that if and when the robber is caught, the case file lands on my desk. I would enjoy working on a matter with some creativity attached to it."

"I hope, if it comes to that point, that you get the case too," Cal said. I thought it was sweet of him to say so.

He stood to leave. "You must excuse me. I am off to make my rounds. I will alert the police if I see any tall women wearing six-inch heels and brandishing nail files."

We both laughed, and Cal took off down the sidewalk at a slow jog.

I finished my wine and shook Ralph's leash. "C'mon, buddy. We're going shopping."

We were back at my condo an hour later. I was lugging two bags from Saks. I would have gone for three, but we were ejected from the store when Ralph took a whiz on a fake potted palm. I didn't blame him. I thought it was the store's fault. Putting a fake plant in a store patronized by dogs was clearly a form of entrapment.

CHAPTER SEVEN

The weekend passed uneventfully but pleasantly. Saturday night Joyce and I went to her son's piano recital, where he faultlessly executed a mini-version of Gershwin's *Rhapsody in Blue*. Sunday morning I attended services at a nearby Presbyterian church that I was thinking of joining.

Many—okay, most—of my friends and colleagues reacted with disbelief if not downright shock when they found out that not only was I a churchgoer, but the church I went to did not include fire dancing and human sacrifice as sacraments. Admittedly there were times when I thought human sacrifice might be appropriate, provided I was the one who got to choose the human to be sacrificed, but the fact was that both my parents were Presbyterians, and except for a brief period of wild rebellion in college during which I attended a Lutheran church, I had always been one of the "frozen chosen" too.

The Phoenix church was just the right size, had adequate air-conditioning, and served Starbucks coffee during the post-service social hour. Most important, although I had visited there several times, no one had asked me to volunteer for anything. The church therefore met my limited but nonnegotiable criteria.

I spent the rest of Sunday reading the paper and drinking coffee. True to his word, Cal had done my laundry Saturday and left it neatly folded at my door.

Monday came as a shock to my system, as Mondays usually did. I managed to drag myself into the office by eight thirty and got in a good hour and a half of work before MJ and Sam appeared at my door for our ten o'clock meeting. MJ showed no signs of having gotten a new piercing, so I figured she'd had a pretty good weekend. Sam was wearing an obviously new pair of shoes and a new silk shirt, so his weekend looked to have included a shopping day.

"Nice shirt," I commented. "Beige looks good on you."

"It's ecru, not beige," Sam corrected. "But thanks. Like my shoes? They're also new."

Evidently I was expected to comment on *all* new articles of apparel.

"Spiffy. Very spiffy," I said, half-standing and peering over my desk at his shoes. Sam preened.

"You didn't say anything about my outfit," grumbled MJ.

They were like two kids vying for their mother's attention. I smiled indulgently and inspected MJ's tight neon green miniskirt, red plaid shirt, and blue leggings. It was kind of a "stoned preppy" look.

"You definitely stand out in the crowd," I told her. Ambiguous but truthful. It seemed to satisfy her.

Keeping a nervous eye on the door (I had forgotten to pick up a doorstop), I quickly outlined the situation Sam and I had discussed last Friday. After MJ was up to speed, we started to strategize about what, if anything, we should do.

"We could castrate Rantwist when he isn't looking," MJ offered.

Sam crossed his legs reflexively. "Bad weekend with the boyfriend?" he asked.

"No. I just think castration is underrated and underused. It's a great deterrent and it's cost effective. No special training required."

Sam stared at her incredulously. "Maybe we should be talking about how to handle you, not Rantwist."

"Now, now, children. Let's not fight," I interjected. "While your suggestion is … um … interesting, MJ, I think we need a more subtle approach. We should collect more hard evidence against Rantwist and find others who will back us up and not cover for him. Once we have our ducks in order we can blow the whistle on him. So far it's just our word against his. He can explain away a few improper charges as simple mistakes. But no way can he explain the systematic imposition of a multitude of such charges."

MJ and Sam nodded in agreement.

"Our starting point will be to find out how many of these weird cases are around and which attorneys they're assigned to. Once we have a list, we'll split it up and talk to each of the attorneys on the list as well as their staff members and try to feel out how many of them are willing to stand up to Rantwist."

"Then we'll all click the heels of our little red shoes together and go home," said Sam sardonically.

MJ gave him a sharp poke with her elbow. "I can check the computer system for arraignments involving suspicious charges," she volunteered. "It's gonna take time, though. Everything that comes into this office is scanned onto the computer, so I hafta wade through a lot of crap."

I silently congratulated myself. This was probably the first time MJ had been inspired to volunteer for anything.

Not to be outdone, Sam shook off his lapse into cynicism and jumped in. "I can check the investigation files for out of the ordinary cases and talk to the other investigators."

"Perfect," I said, smiling at them like a proud parent.

We agreed to reconvene in my office the next day at the same time to compare notes on what we'd found out. Before we went our separate ways, I emphasized the need to keep our plans secret, even from friends and family. I didn't want Rantwist or Alan to catch wind of what we were doing until we were fully prepared for a confrontation. I felt like the head of a secret club. All we needed were matching code rings.

Since I had nothing to do on our super-secret investigation until MJ and Sam put their lists together, I got back to the less exciting but necessary task of drafting responses to a stack of defense motions. I worked without interruption until the lobby receptionist buzzed me just before noon.

"You got time to meet with a member of the sheriff's department?" she asked.

I was planning to head out to lunch, but I couldn't pass up the opportunity to meet someone who actually asked for permission to see me instead of barging into my office unannounced.

"Why not," I said.

"Great. His name's Deputy Bryan Turner. I'll send him on up."

I had heard of Bryan Turner. He was the second in command at the sheriff's department. The sheriff was usually out shaking hands and raising campaign funds, so that meant that, for all intents and purposes, Turner ran the day-to-day operations of the department.

A polite knock sounded at the door. This guy was too good to be true.

"Come in," I said, my voice a bit shaky with emotion.

A man in a deputy's uniform entered and extended his hand in greeting. "Hi. I'm Bryan Turner, Ms. Williams. Thanks for taking the time to meet with me on such short notice."

"Urk." It was the best I could manage in return. Not only was Deputy Turner polite, but he was extremely good looking; wavy blond hair, blue eyes, tall, well built, the whole package. I reflexively looked for a wedding ring. No ring. But these days that could mean he was gay and/or unmarried, or married but liked to play around on the side. I tried again to dazzle him with my wit. "Uh, nice to meet you, Mr. Turner." Not brilliant, but better than *urk*. "Please, have a seat. What can I do for you?"

Bryan sat down and the chair wondrously made none of the usual creaking, groaning, and cracking noises.

"I heard you're the new attorney assigned to Major Felonies. I head up the major crimes division at the sheriff's department. Nine times out of ten my guys are the arresting officers on the cases assigned to you. I thought it made sense for me to get acquainted and make myself available to you to answer any questions you might have on specific cases or generally on how our departments work together." His delivery was smooth and practiced. I figured this was a standard PR visit with the new attorney.

Interesting, though; so Bryan was the arresting officer, or at least was in charge of the arresting officers, responsible for the great Third and Central Avenue exhibitionist bust. That must have been a feather in his cap, what with all the romance and danger. Imagine; busting an unarmed half-naked guy whose most threatening behavior was to scream out to jeering passersby, "Do not judge, lest ye be judged yourself. Besides, it's cold outside," as he was hauled into the squad car. As an aside, it was in fact about a hundred and eight degrees outside at the time of the arrest. I think he just felt pressured to offer some defense to the abusive commentary of passing drivers on the size of his penis.

"Yes. In fact, I was just speaking to my staff this morning about a matter sent over by the charging division in which your department made the arrest. The charge seemed excessive," I said.

"Probably drug related. We make more felony drug arrests than any other kind. It goes through cycles. For a while, cocaine was the hot property; now it's crystal meth. It's either made locally or comes up from Mexico. The sad, really sad, part is that at least fifty percent of the crystal meth arrests are referred to juvenile court because the defendant is under eighteen years old."

I didn't know whether Turner was being intelligently politic and avoiding the subject or was out of the loop on what MJ, Sam, and I had begun referring to as our "special files." I decided to feel him out a bit more on the subject and find out where he was coming from. "Actually, I haven't gotten any drug cases. Not a one. I do have a couple of adultery cases, an exhibitionism case, and a case involving public masturbation."

He looked confused for a second and then laughed. "I get it. Rantwist's letting you settle in a bit. I guess he wants you to handle some misdemeanors until you get your feet wet."

I stared at him darkly. "First, I practiced in criminal law in Chicago for fourteen years before I came here. My feet are not just wet, they are sopping wet and smelly." I realized too late that that didn't come out right. The *sopping wet* part made sense, but *smelly*? I needed to work on my rhetoric. "Okay, maybe not smelly, but you get the idea."

Turner nodded and stifled a grin. Damn him.

I plunged ahead. "As for the files to which I just alluded, each involves a charge of first or second degree felony."

Turner looked at me sardonically. "I seriously think Rantwist must be having a bit of fun with you."

"That occurred to me. I asked him about one of the cases, and he's dead serious about the charge. I also found out that at least two other attorneys in my division have gotten files involving overcharged crimes."

"Have they spoken to Rantwist about it?"

"No. The general opinion thus far has been that Rantwist is just another county attorney to be humored until his term is up, and job security trumps conscientious professionalism."

"Sadly, that last part sounds about right. The average tenure of a county attorney is four years. After the first term, they usually either get dumped by the voters or run for a more exalted office, like attorney general or governor. It isn't nearly as bad in my department. Sheriff Hal has been in office for twelve years, and he'll probably be there for another twelve years. Even though he's sixty-seven years old, he doesn't show any signs of slowing down."

I'd heard about Hal Harmon long before I'd come to Arizona. He was a national celebrity and a folk hero. Nicknamed "Hard Hal," Sheriff Hal had cracked down on crimes, especially drug-related crimes, and was a tireless advocate for law and order. He always wore a white cowboy hat. The hat combined with his height of six feet five inches made him immediately recognizable at the many functions he attended. His detractors said he was a publicity hound, but the public adored him, and his approval ratings were consistently high.

"Listen," said Turner abruptly. "Would you mind giving me the defendant's name in the exhibitionist case? I can take a look at it from my end and find out if a felony arrest was made initially, or if the felony charge came out of your office's charging division. "

I could guess the answer to that question. Rantwist was on a personal crusade against evil. I doubted the sheriff's department had anything to do with Larkin's overcharge. Nevertheless, I made it a policy never to turn down an offer of help by a good-looking man.

"The defendant's name is Larry Larkin," I said. "By the way, Mr. Turner, while you're at it, could you also find out where all the drug cases are going? They certainly aren't coming to me."

"Will do, and please, call me Bryan."

He smiled charmingly and stood to leave.

"Thanks, Bryan, and please call me Kate." Kate of the smelly feet. Damn, sometimes I can be such an idiot.

"I'll get back to you later today on all this stuff," he said as he shook my hand. "In the meantime, please feel free to give me a call if you have any other questions or need help with something."

I smiled back at him. "I will, and thank you so much for coming by." I could be charming too. I just needed a little more lead time to prepare.

CHAPTER EIGHT

I was still sitting at my desk with a foolish smile on my face when MJ came in a few minutes later.

"I heard a rumor that Bryan Turner came to see you."

News really traveled fast in this office.

"I can tell by the asinine smile on your face that it's true."

I wiped the asinine smile off my face. "Did you come to see me for a reason other than to check my visitor schedule?"

MJ snickered. "Somebody's got low blood sugar. Don't get your butt in a bundle. The first time I saw Bryan, I was so distracted by his looks that I walked into the side of the building. It doesn't help either that he's a really nice guy. Someone that good looking should have a lousy personality just to balance things out."

"I've seen better," I lied. "Excuse me, but I need to run out for a sandwich before I faint. We'll have to continue this discussion later, if ever."

MJ seemed oblivious to my attempt to put her off. "Perfect. I was going to pick up some lunch too. I'll go with you. You paying?"

I sighed. I knew I shouldn't encourage this kind of behavior, but I was too hungry to argue, and it would be nice to have some company. "Fine. Whatever. At some point, though, you're going to have to spring for lunch."

"Come on. You get paid the big bucks. I barely make enough to cover my rent."

"Then move to a place you can afford."

"Why didn't I think of that? I'll have my stuff moved into the parking garage as soon as we get back from lunch. I'm thinking space forty-five would be good. It has the best view."

"You could find a better-paying job, you know."

"True, but what other employer would let me express my individual style the way I do here? One must make financial sacrifices to preserve one's integrity," MJ said sanctimoniously.

I thought *What do piercings, tattoos, and neon miniskirts have to do with integrity?*

We decided on Cutie's Sub Shop because it was close, thus requiring minimal exposure to the furnace outside.

The line at the counter was fairly long, even though it was past the noon rush hour. When it was finally our turn to order, I got a cheese sandwich and a Diet Coke. MJ ordered a twelve-inch meatball sub with extra cheese, two bags of chips, and a chocolate shake so large the plastic cup it was served in could be upended and used as an end table. We found a small table in the back, which was no easy feat in the crowded restaurant. I watched in fascination as MJ removed the top half of her sandwich bun, dumped both bags of chips on the cheese covered meatballs, then replaced the bun and squished down. She demolished the whole thing before I was halfway through my own much smaller sandwich.

She wiped her mouth with a napkin, sighed with satisfaction, and settled back in her chair to enjoy her shake. "In answer to your question, yes," she said between sips.

I looked at her blankly. "What question?"

"Yes, I did come to see you for a reason other than to check up on your visitor schedule. I wanted to tell you something I heard. It probably has nothing to do with our special files, but it's just really weird."

She paused to suck on her straw.

"Go on," I said impatiently.

"Calm down. You can't rush milk shakes. They need to be savored."

This from a woman who'd just inhaled a twelve-inch sub.

I waited until she finished her drink and noisily vacuumed the bottom of the cup with her straw. She threw the empty cup over the heads of the adjacent diners into a trash bin next to the door.

"Nice shot," I commented.

"I've done better. That one ricocheted a little off the rim." MJ then delicately used her little finger to remove a food particle wedged between her back molars. She settled back in her chair with a contented sigh, and was ready to talk.

"I ran into Jenny Rolly in the file room." In response to my raised eyebrow, she explained. "Jenny is the paralegal assigned to the misdemeanor crimes group. Since they just deal with misdemeanors, which aren't too complicated, they only have one paralegal for the whole group. Jenny's got a pretty good deal most of the time. Most of the cases are cookie cutter, and there's hardly ever any motions filed.

"But Jenny says that lately she's been run ragged trying to keep up with a huge load of drug cases. They always have a pretty steady stream of misdemeanor possession cases in Jenny's area, but she says this latest batch involves some pretty big deals. Yet all the defendants are charged with misdemeanors. She figured maybe they were part of a bigger bust and had agreed to give testimony in exchange for reduced charges. They've gotten cases like that off and on in the past. But she couldn't find anything in the files saying that's what happened. She went to one of the attorneys she works for and asked him what was going on, but he just brushed her off. Jenny wondered if we knew anything about it. Do we?"

"No, we don't," I said. "I need a cookie." Cookies are my source of strength and inspiration.

"I'll have chocolate chip," said MJ.

I cut in at the front of the line at the counter and ordered two chocolate-chip cookies. When it comes to cookies, there is no such thing as delayed gratification in my book. The counter clerk, a nervous young man who had just started his shift, said something about me needing to wait my turn but didn't push the issue when I shot him an icy look.

I returned to our table, and we munched on our cookies thoughtfully. MJ was the first to break the silence. She was also the first to finish her cookie.

"Nope. I get nothing. None of it makes any sense. If Rantwist is a law-and-order guy, why would he lighten up on drug felonies? I mean, sure, maybe he's got a big bug up his ass about sex offenses, so he comes down extra hard on them. But that doesn't fit with going soft on drug crimes."

I licked some chocolate off my finger. "The attorney Jenny spoke to in her department doesn't seem to think it's a big deal. Maybe it isn't. Maybe the information on the reduced charges is in files kept in another department, and they haven't been transferred over to the misdemeanor division yet."

MJ snorted. "Lemme tell you something about the attorneys in the misdemeanor division. You've got two types. First, you've got the ones who are fresh out of law school and are friggin' ignorant. We had to put a buddy system in place to cut down on the number of them that get lost on the way to the courthouse. The other day one of them asked me if it was okay to wear tennis shorts to court. Can you imagine? Tennis shorts."

I forbore from mentioning that MJ was hardly one to criticize the fashion sense of others, although the idea of tennis shorts in court was pretty ludicrous.

"Another one of them," she continued, "invited her whole family to watch her first court appearance. It was a just a sentencing hearing, and all she had to do was stand there and say, 'The state has no objection,' when the judge asked the parties if they both agreed to the plea. Her family whistled and applauded after she delivered her one lousy line. The judge held everyone in contempt. Then there was the time ..."

MJ was on a roll.

"I get it, I get it," I interrupted. "Continue with your point."

MJ looked nonplussed. Apparently she'd lost track of her original point. I reminded her. "You said there were *two* types of attorneys in the misdemeanors division?"

"Oh yeah. Okay, so the second type is the burnouts from Major Felonies who just want to slide until retirement."

Great. That's encouraging, I thought. Was that what was in store for me in a few years? I would become a burnout handling shoplifting and DUIs?

"Boiled down, what you're saying is that you don't think the attorneys in Misdemeanors have the intelligence and/or the interest to pick up on the undercharged cases."

"Bingo," said MJ, smacking the table with the flat of her hand. The counter clerk jumped and looked at us nervously. I smiled at him, pointed to MJ and made a circular motion around my ear with my index finger. My attempt at levity did not appear to make him any less tense. He continued to watch MJ fearfully.

"What's the deal?" I asked. "Do you and the counter clerk have a history? At most, your table banging should prompt a startled glance. But that guy still looks scared."

MJ turned her head to look at him and gave him a little wave. He flinched.

"Oh," she said turning back to me. "That's my boyfriend, Mitchie."

I looked from MJ to the acned young man behind the counter and back again. He was half her size and half her age. Aside from a noticeable facial tic, which I had a feeling would disappear as soon as MJ left, he looked pretty normal, albeit a tad on the nerdy side.

This was the guy she'd pierced her nose over?

MJ must have guessed what I was thinking, because she said, "You can't tell by looking at him, but he's really intense, and he's great in bed."

I briefly wondered how in the world you *could* tell if a guy was good in bed just by looking at him. Several possibilities flashed through my mind, all of which were X-rated.

"I guess we'd better head back to work," I said, shutting down my mental slide show.

"Sure. But I gotta introduce you to Mitchie first."

Fortunately, the shop was still busy enough to prevent more than a brief exchange of how-do-you-dos between Mitchie and me, because I really did need to get back to work. I had plenty of cases to worry about in addition to the special files, which now included Jenny's undercharged drug cases.

CHAPTER NINE

Before MJ and I parted company in the lobby of our building, I asked if she could get me a copy of one of the files Jenny had described so I could check out the situation for myself. MJ promised to have one on my desk by the end of the day.

I bumped into Alan, literally, as he was leaving my office. The stains on his tie, suit, and shirt had multiplied. He looked like he'd been in a food fight. I checked to make sure none of his mobile buffet had gotten on me.

"Oh, there you are. Taking a long lunch?" he asked, pointedly staring at his wristwatch.

"Actually, I was taking a *late* lunch," I answered. "Did you need something?"

"You had lunch alone?" he asked nonresponsively.

It's none of your business whether I went to lunch alone or with the cast of Cats, I thought. I decided to keep things civilized, though.

"I had lunch with MJ. I really do need to get back to work now. Unless you have something to discuss that is time sensitive, could I just call you later, and you can tell me whatever it is you came here to tell me?"

"You and MJ are turning into quite the good buddies," he said.

"Leave." So much for civilized.

"Actually, the County Attorney sent me down to ask if you could spare a moment to talk to him."

Why, oh why does Rantwist keep sending his messenger boy instead of contacting me directly? I have a cell phone, office phone, e-mail, and a fax. Surely one of these provides a more efficient means of communication.

"Is it urgent?" I asked.

Alan smirked. "I don't mean to tell you how to do your job," he said condescendingly, "but I believe if the County Attorney wishes to see you, you should comply immediately with his request regardless of your personal preference for a different meeting time. He is, after all, the County Attorney."

I reminded myself that the law frowned upon murder. Still, even after considering the negative legal consequences, it was a tough decision not to smack Alan over the head with a chair. The deciding factor was that the chair was in such bad shape, it would probably disintegrate on impact and merely wound him.

"I'll give Stan a call and see what he wants," I said.

Alan looked rattled. "That's not part of the protocol," he said nervously.

"So amend the protocol." I slipped around Alan, who had parked himself squarely in the center of my doorway. Fortunately, he was such a wimpy little shit, there was enough room for me to get past without having to brush up against him.

He tried to grab the phone from me as I punched in Stan's extension. My call went through, and Stan picked up immediately.

"County Attorney Stan Rantwist," he boomed.

"Stan, this is Kate Williams. I've got Alan here in my office, and he says you need to speak with me. Is it something we can discuss over the phone?"

"Hey, Kate. How're you doing?" Stan was in good-ol'-boy mode. "Say hi to Alan for me."

I looked over at Alan. "Stan says hi," I said.

"Listen, Katie, I would prefer for you to come up to my office. I like to see people's faces when I talk to them; gives me a better feel for what they're thinking. A lot of times people don't say what they think."

It's a good thing he couldn't see my face at that moment, because it had "you're an ass" written all over it.

"When would be a good time for you?" I asked through clenched teeth.

"No time like the present—haw haw haw. See ya in a few." Click.

He didn't even have the courtesy to ask if I was busy. I thought, *I really need to update my résumé.*

"Lead the way, Alan," I growled. I avoided looking at his face, which I was sure bore a smug expression. I took one last wistful glance at the chair-*cum*-weapon as we left my office.

Alan, perhaps sensing he was living on borrowed time, neither said anything nor hummed during our trip to Rantwist's office.

I walked past Beth, who didn't bother looking up from the women's magazine she was reading, and knocked on Rantwist's door. Fuck protocol.

"Come in," snapped Rantwist. He was off good-ol'-boy mode.

He looked surprised when I walked in. "Oh, it's you, Katie. I thought it was Beth. I usually require that visitors check in with her before seeing me," he said by way of apology, or accusation; I couldn't tell which. In any event, it appeared he'd changed his former position and was enforcing all the rules of protocol.

"Never you mind, though. Y'all come on in and take a seat."

Snap. Back to good ol' boy. This guy was smooth; schizophrenic, but smooth.

I slammed the door in Alan's face, not that it would do any good. He would find a way to get in.

Rantwist looked pointedly at my shoes and cleared his throat. I was on the brink of breaching yet another one of the rules of protocol. I removed my shoes and then walked across the floor and sat in the same chair I'd occupied before.

"So did Alan tell y'all why I wanted to speak with you?" asked Rantwist.

"No, we didn't have a chance to talk," said Alan. He was standing behind me. I wasn't surprised.

"Let me get right to the point then," said Rantwist.

Too late. You've already wasted enough of my time. Getting right to the point is no longer an option, I groused to myself.

"Alan here tells me that your paralegal, MJ, has been asking questions about certain cases assigned to you for prosecution." Stan's voice had developed a slight edge. "One of them is the Larkin case you asked me about last week."

I settled back in my chair and smiled thinly. "I believe asking questions about and doing research on my cases is part of MJ's job."

"She's asking the wrong kind of questions, and she's talking to the wrong people: people who have nothing to do with any of your cases. She's asking about certain special files that I assigned to a trusted few in the office, including you."

Interesting, I thought. *Rantwist also refers to them as "special files." He's obviously aware that they're out of the ordinary.*

"I was the one responsible for hiring you, because I believed you could best further The Cause. I entrusted you with a sacred task. I want you to control your staff and prosecute these cases to the best of your ability. Do you understand? I cannot tolerate any sign of disloyalty." Rantwist was clearly agitated now. He visibly shook, and the strands of hair wrapped around his head started to unwind *en masse*.

I wanted to tell him where to shove his special files. I wanted to strangle him with his greasy strands. Instead, I forced myself to breathe slowly and stay calm. If I quit in a huff or provoked him into firing me, he would just replace me with someone more compliant, and his nutty crusade would continue, to the detriment of people who, though not innocent of any crimes, were not guilty of the charges leveled against them. I was more determined than ever not to let Rantwist get away with it.

I forced my visage into what I hoped was a doglike expression of fealty that completely belied my inner dialogue. I prayed he wasn't as good at reading faces as he claimed. Fortunately, he was momentarily distracted by the uncooperative hair clump from hell and was trying to plaster it back in place.

"Sir, I understand your position completely. I will speak to MJ and make sure she stays on task." It wasn't exactly a lie; I didn't say *which* task.

Rantwist, having made a further mess of his hair, which, in defiance of the laws of gravity, now stood up on the top of his head like a deformed horn, said, "See that you do, and to help you stay on the path, I have asked Alan to review your team's work for a while."

"Certainly, sir. Will that be all, sir?" I said brightly. My teeth started to hurt from all the clenching, and I had a bad headache as a result of all the anger I was suppressing. I wondered if anyone in the building had cookies.

Rantwist dismissed me with an imperious wave of his hand. I all but curtsied before I left his office. Thankfully, Alan did not follow me. He and Rantwist probably had other business to talk about—like whether to ask for the death penalty in a jaywalking case.

The strain must have shown on my face, because Beth asked, "Are you okay?"

I nodded, but I must not have been very convincing.

"Don't worry, sweetie. Just hang in there. They come and they go," she said reassuringly.

"You mean county attorneys?" I asked, although I was pretty sure that's what she meant.

"Indeed. As for the current holder of the office, you shouldn't have to wait too long before he's gone. He's definitely a one-termer."

I looked at Beth curiously. "Why do you say that?"

"Because he's a nut," she said calmly.

Beth had held the position of executive assistant to the county attorney for as long as anyone could remember, weathering wildly diverse administrations. The staff attributed her longevity to either impenetrable serenity or undetectable insanity. Nothing and no one seemed to faze her.

"You've noticed?" I asked wearily.

"Helen Keller would notice. Have a cookie." She opened her desk drawer and, miracle of miracles, pulled out a plate of homemade chocolate chip cookies.

I took a cookie, but continued to gaze longingly at the plate.

Beth said, "Have two."

I loved this woman. I took another cookie and thanked her profusely.

"You're more than welcome, my dear," she said. "Now you'd better skedaddle, because that little weasel Alan is bound to come out of Stan's office any moment now. One look at him and you'll 'lose your cookies.'"

I smiled in appreciation of Beth's joke, then took her advice and skedaddled.

CHAPTER TEN

I plunked down in my chair and mentally reviewed what had just happened in Rantwist's office. I was getting used to his reprimands and not-so-subtle threats. What bugged me was that he said I was one of the chosen ones to whom he'd entrusted some of the special files, and he had hired me expressly for that purpose.

Was there something in my résumé that implied I was moronically loyal to wacko employers? Or did I just make that sort of impression on people? Thinking about it was leading me dangerously close to in-depth reflection. I needed a distraction, and fast.

I put in calls to MJ and Sam, but neither of them answered. I left voice-mail messages for both asking them to come to a meeting in my office at four o'clock that afternoon. It was already three, which wasn't giving them much prior notice, but, in light of my conversation with Rantwist, I wanted to give them a heads-up as soon as possible.

I managed to prepare for an oral argument on an evidentiary motion scheduled for the next morning, although I couldn't have said how. I was still angry with Rantwist, and anger is a tough emotion to work around.

Neither MJ nor Sam got back to me. I was afraid they hadn't picked up my messages in time. But at four o'clock on the dot Sam marched in and sat down. MJ shuffled in a few minutes later. She muttered something about Sam's lack of chivalry—at least I think she was referring to Sam—and left. A minute later she returned, dragging an extra chair from the empty office next to mine. Once she was seated, she and Sam looked at me expectantly. I closed the door before I spoke.

"I was summonsed to Rantwist's office today. He heard MJ was asking questions around the office about the special files. That's what he called them too: the special files." I looked at MJ. "He pretty much threatened to fire me if I didn't bring you back in line." Then, addressing both of them, I said, "He made it very clear again that we need to prosecute the special files assigned to us forthwith, no questions asked."

MJ and Sam did not appear to be at all surprised or worried.

"There's more," I continued. "Alan's going to review our work for a while."

Again, minimal reaction from MJ and Sam.

"In other words, nothing much has changed, right? Rantwist is still demented and Alan is still a sleaze," said MJ.

MJ had pretty much summed things up: nothing much had changed. Rantwist had warned me last Friday not to question his master plan. The only thing new was that this afternoon Stan had included MJ in his warning by name. As for Alan, he was already such a snoop that it was difficult to imagine what he could do to step things up.

"If you guys are okay with it, I want to keep doing what we're doing. I want to nail Rantwist. I still believe there have to be others willing to stand up against him. Good lord, even his own secretary thinks he's a nut case. Once we have the evidence and the witnesses, we can take the matter to law enforcement, the press, the public—anyone who can bring attention to the issue and pressure Rantwist into backing off of his idiot cause.

"By the way, that reminds me. I spoke with Bryan Turner from the sheriff's department today …"

"He's so cute!" MJ and Sam exclaimed in unison.

I ignored the interruption. "I think Bryan may be able to help us get information from the sheriff's department about the undercharged drug cases in the misdemeanor division. At least he *said* I could call him if I had any questions or needed help. We'll see if he means it."

Sam had a dreamy look in his eyes. I snapped my fingers in his face. "Focus, Sam."

MJ shook her head slightly. "It won't do any good," she said. "Sam's got a thing for Bryan. He won't be back on the planet for at least another minute or so."

A thought struck me. "Um … does Bryan, er … date men?"

"Nah. Bryan's thoroughly hetero," said MJ. "He's dated half the women in this building, and he's working on the other half. I hear he doesn't consider marriage a deterrent."

Damn. The best date prospect I'd met in Phoenix so far was a player. I'd almost rather he was gay. At least then we could still hang out as friends. But based upon past experience, no way would I ever date a player again. Nothing hurts a woman's self-esteem more than to discover she is in no way special but is just another female in a long string of conquests.

I snapped my fingers in Sam's face again. "Sam!" I said sternly.

His eyes slowly regained focus. "You know," he said, "I could talk to Bryan if you want. There's this little café on First Avenue where we could meet. It has cozy, private little booths …" He started to get that misty look again.

"Sam!" shouted MJ. Both Sam and I jumped. "Earth to Sam. Dammit. We gotta find you a man. Good sex will help your concentration at work. Trust me. That's the only reason I function at all in this dump."

An unwanted image of MJ and Mitchie popped into my head.

"*I* will talk to Bryan," I said firmly. I thought I heard Sam mutter "bitch" under his breath, but I wasn't sure.

"Did you need to talk to us about anything else?" asked MJ, glancing at the clock.

"Yes. Just one more thing." I paused, unsure how to proceed. "Rantwist mentioned that he'd selected me specially to handle some of his special files. He said, more or less, that I was one of the chosen ones entrusted to carry out his plans. Do I give off the impression that I'd be good for that kind of job?"

Sam and MJ burst out laughing. I failed to see the humor.

Wiping her eyes, MJ choked out "You obviously don't give us that impression. You've spent most of the past few days plotting how to expose your boss as a lunatic."

"I think Rantwist had another reason for hiring you," said Sam, who had sobered after appearing to realize that I was seriously concerned. "Take a look at the facts: You've never practiced Arizona law before, you're from out of town, so you have no local connections to speak of, and you haven't built up any kind of a reputation here yet. You're the perfect choice. You're a good attorney, but you have no local creds. You pointed out yourself that if you blew the whistle on Rantwist, it would be his word against yours, and your word isn't enough."

Sam was right. I was actually relieved to think that Rantwist had hired me not because I had a spectacular character flaw but because I was alone and powerless.

"What about you guys?" I asked. "You're part of my team. Why did he think he could trust you to be quiet?"

MJ and Sam again looked amused. Sam spoke up. "You no doubt have noticed that this is a very structured organization. Paralegals and investigators report to the attorney or attorneys they're assigned to. Going over the head of your boss is a no-no. Further, this is a government agency; ergo, independent thinking is frowned upon. Pretty much anyone who's been here longer than six months has learned to ask few questions, lie low, and avoid responsibility for everything, the last of which is accomplished by following orders, period. That way, if something goes wrong, you can blame your boss."

I was really getting tired of hearing this. I'd gotten the same message from every staff member I'd talked to thus far and had heard it twice now from Sam.

"Is that what you and MJ are doing? Just following my orders?"

"In our case, mine and MJ's I mean, I think Rantwist believes we have the employee mentality I just described, but he also understands that, to the rest of the staff, we are outsiders. To point out the obvious, MJ dresses a bit oddly and has a bit of an attitude problem ..."

"Hey, I do not," MJ objected. "My fashion sense is ahead of its time, and I don't have an attitude problem. I basically just don't give a fuck."

"Point made," sighed Sam. "As for me, well, let's just say that most of the male staff are uncomfortable around me. That being the case, MJ and I have even fewer friends and even less credibility than you in this office. No one is going to believe us, and no one is going to take our side. As for us 'just following orders,' I think I am speaking for MJ as well as myself when I say that we actually think a lot of you. Our ... um ... idiosyncrasies don't seem to bother you. What matters to you is how we do our job and whether we—I mean all of us now—are doing the right thing."

MJ nodded emphatically in agreement.

I was touched by MJ and Sam's fealty, but that aside, what Sam said made sense. It was painful to admit we were the Odd Squad of the office, though.

"You know, all this may work to our advantage," I said optimistically "If Rantwist thinks he's convinced me to toe the line, and I certainly left him with that impression, and he doesn't consider any of us a real threat, then we can keep asking questions and trying to recruit supporters, provided we are a little more careful to stay under the radar." *I was starting to sound like Siever now.* "Siccing Alan on us is not much of a threat to our investigation. We can handle him." I smiled fondly at MJ and Sam. "Rantwist underestimated your intelligence and integrity, and that's what's going to bring him down."

They smiled back at me.

"So go home, you two," I ordered. "Enjoy the rest of your evening. And thanks for being so frank with me." I really meant it too. This unlikely pair was turning out to be a pretty good team.

MJ slipped a file on my desk just before she left. "From the misdemeanor division," she said. "I tried to make a copy, but too many people were in the copy room. Just make sure you get it back to me first thing tomorrow morning so I can put it back before anyone notices." I thanked her and tucked the file into my briefcase.

CHAPTER ELEVEN

I decided to take the stairs when I left rather than risk running into Alan on the elevator. Alan struck me as the type who never took the stairs. The guy could really use a few trips to the gym, not to mention a new wardrobe, a dry cleaner, some dandruff shampoo, deodorant and mouthwash.

As usual, Ralph met me at the door when I got home. Yes, Ralph ate too much, pooped and peed too much, and shed too much, but he adored me unconditionally. If Ralph were a man, I would buy him diapers, give him a razor, and marry him.

I only took time to change my shoes before taking Ralph out for his walk. Even though I was home on time, even a little bit early, Ralph had the frantic expression he always wore when he really had to pee bad.

Macy came out of her condo just as I stepped outside mine. "Hey, Ms. hot-shot attorney. How's it going?"

"Hi, Macy. I'm doing okay, but I don't have time to talk. Ralph needs to go outside ASAP."

"No problem, sweetie. I'll walk with you. I relate to what Ralph is going through. My doctor's got me on a lot of them—whadayacall 'em—diuretics. I gotta pee all the time. Hey, I know; if I get the urge along the way, maybe Ralph and I can both lift a leg on a tree. Or maybe we can get creative and come up with some kinda fountain motif."

"Pardon?" I asked, I think understandably.

Macy got on the elevator with me. "You know, like in Rome, where they got those fountains that look like angels peeing. I figure if you gotta go, why not make an artistic statement while you're at it?"

I smiled but wondered whether Macy was taking more than just diuretics.

Once we were out on the sidewalk, Macy asked, "So, how're you getting along with the *shmegege* these days?"

"What's a *shmegege?*"

Macy chuckled. "It's Yiddish. It means 'idiot.' I'm talking about your boss, the county attorney; or should I call him the county apostle?"

Great word, *shmegege*. I needed to remember that one.

"Things are about the same," I sighed. "He's still on a religious quest, and I'm still thinking of leaving."

"What *thinking*? Why don't you just quit? You're a smart girl. You can find a job anywhere. In fact, you should set up your own shop. Who needs a boss?"

"I'm just not sure," I said, shaking my head.

"You're a glutton for punishment, that's what you are. You're not gonna change this schmuck. Why don't you leak to the press what he's doing? Let public opinion take him down."

"Don't think I haven't thought about it," I sighed. "I guess I was hoping to get more people on my side before I took that kind of step. Rantwist's a powerful man."

"What if I do it? Who's to say you're even involved? I don't gotta say where I got the information."

From behind us came a hearty "Halloo!" Both Macy and I jumped. Ralph, who was in midstream, lowered his leg but kept peeing.

Cal jogged up to us. "Sorry. I didn't mean to startle you," he said, looking down at Ralph, who was now sitting in a pool of pee.

Macy looked adoringly at Cal. "Why, Calvin," she simpered, "how nice to see you. Lovely day, isn't it?"

It was over a hundred degrees, and we were all sweating. Cal in particular. How anyone could jog in this heat was beyond me.

Cal gave Macy a perfunctory nod and turned his attention to me. "How's the prosecution business these days?" he asked.

I started to say "good," but Macy cut me off. "How do you think it's going? She works for a *meshugener,* a crazy person." Gone was the simpering tone. Macy clearly did not like being ignored.

Cal stopped jogging in place and looked at me questioningly. "What's she talking about?"

I sighed. "I'm having a bit of a problem with someone at work," I said.

"Is there anything I can do to help? I don't know any of the people you work with, but I've got a lot of experience with other people in your field. I know the mentality."

"Tell you what," I said. "Why don't we all go up to my condo and have a drink. I really could use some help sorting things out, and God knows I could use a drink."

"Sure," said Cal. "Is Ralph through doing his stuff though?"

We all looked down at Ralph. The urine had already evaporated, and he seemed at peace with the world.

"He's fine," I said. "He needs a bath, but he's fine."

Macy put her hands on her hips and lifted her chin. "I'd love to join you, dear, provided Mr. Jenkins does not object." Macy's diction was unusually clipped and formal.

Cal glanced at her. "I don't mind," he said after a pause. The pause was a mistake. Macy looked like she wanted to strangle him.

I put my arm around Macy and said soothingly "We need to get out of this heat. We're all a bit cranky."

"Don't make excuses for him," grumbled Macy, but she allowed me to guide her back to the elevator. Cal and Ralph trailed behind us.

Once we were inside my condo, I had Ralph lie in the foyer and told Cal and Macy to make themselves at home while I changed out of my work clothes. Cal and Macy looked around doubtfully. My condo's furnishings were on the sparse side. I sold or gave away most of the furniture in my Chicago apartment and hadn't gotten around to buying new furniture yet. My living room furnishings consisted of a TV perched on a wood packing crate and an old red crushed-velvet couch left by the previous owner. Since it was their only choice, Macy and Cal sat on the couch. They sat at opposite ends and stared straight ahead. They were still sitting and staring when I emerged from my bedroom a few minutes later in jeans and a tank top.

"Can I get you both a drink?" I asked.

"Yes!" they responded in unison.

"Is chardonnay okay? I haven't done any shopping lately"—like in the past month—"so I'm a little low on provisions."

Neither of them looked thrilled at the prospect of white wine. Macy volunteered to retrieve a bottle of scotch from her condo. Cal told her he thought that was a great idea, and Macy smiled at him with real warmth.

I poured myself a glass of wine, hauled a kitchen chair into the living room, and then sat and made small talk with Cal as I sipped my wine. After Macy had been gone about five minutes, we heard clanking in the hallway, then a knock on the door. I held the door open for Macy as she pushed in a bar cart loaded with scotch, gin, and vodka, along with mixers, bowls of chips and pretzels, carrot sticks, three kinds of dip, and a tray of steaming cocktail weenies. Cal jumped up from the couch to help her.

"I brought some munchies in case anyone was hungry," she said breathlessly. "It's just some stuff I had lying around."

It was more stuff than I'd had lying around my kitchen cumulatively for the entire time I'd lived in my condo.

Ralph's ears perked up at the new smells.

"Can I give the doggy a weenie?" asked Macy. "He looks so sad and alone over there. It would cheer him up."

"Sure," I said. Directing my next comment to Ralph, I added, "But *you* are not invited into the living room."

Macy threw Ralph a couple of weenies, which he caught in midair. They were gone in one gulp. Ralph believed chewing was overrated.

Cal and Macy got busy making themselves drinks. I had already poured myself another glass of chardonnay, so I was set.

"Now, what's the deal?" asked Cal, although, because he'd just shoved a handful of pretzels in his mouth, it sounded more like "Gow waf's da deo?"

"You mean what's the deal at my office? How much of it do you want to hear?"

"Allfut," mumbled Cal.

The wine had loosened me up a bit, so I gave a pretty detailed account of what was happening at work, most of which Macy hadn't heard yet either. She clucked sympathetically and murmured, "You poor dear," from time to time throughout my recitation.

Cal said, "So Rantwist's a nut, this Alan guy who works for him is a sleazy nut, and except for you and your staff, no one seems to give a damn."

"That pretty much sums things up," I said.

"What about that Ryan guy?" asked Macy. "He offered to check into his office's records for the guy standing on the corner with his privates hanging out. He might be able to get information easier than you can. Alan don't spy on the sheriff's department too, does he?"

"His name is Bryan Turner, not Ryan. He promised to get me some information on the Larkin case by this afternoon, but I haven't heard back from him yet. Plus, I haven't quite figured out the relationship between the sheriff and the county attorney. The sheriff might be a hundred percent behind what Rantwist is doing for all I know."

"I doubt that," said Cal. "Except for his penchant for publicity, Sheriff Harmon seems like a pretty straight shooter. He plays by the book. Plus, he's been in office for a long time and is close to retirement. Why would he change his modus operandi at this late date and back an upstart like Rantwist? There's nothing in it for him."

Macy was licking her fingers, having polished off the last weenie. "Could it be that the sheriff is so busy making nice at publicity events that he's not paying attention and doesn't know the bad guys his men are arresting aren't being charged right by the county attorney's office?"

"That could be part of it," I said after pausing to give it some thought. "It is true that the arresting officer has nothing to do with the case after it comes to our office unless the case goes to trial, in which event the arresting officer becomes a material witness. So if the special files all plead out, which is how Rantwist wants them handled, there's no reason for the sheriff's people to be involved in the case at all after the arrest."

"You're saying it's possible then that law enforcement is totally out of the loop?" I could tell by the relief in Cal's voice that he was uncomfortable with the idea that anyone from law enforcement might be dirty. He was still an FBI agent at heart.

"You should get hold of this Ryan guy again," said Macy.

"Bryan," I corrected automatically.

"Tell me something: why is it that whenever you mention this Ryan … sorry, I mean Bryan … you blush. It may be the scotch talking, but I think you got a little thing for the guy."

"It's the scotch talking," I retorted icily, but I knew I was blushing as I said it.

Macy rolled her eyes, then asked, "What about my idea of tipping off the newspapers?"

"I don't know. There's no guarantee that the newspapers will follow up on it. I'm sure they get lots of tips every day."

"Not to mention the fact that Rantwist has some pretty powerful friends," Cal interjected. "I remember reading that Albert Kenly is a huge contributor to his campaign."

I looked at him questioningly.

"Kenly's a local land developer, and he's loaded. He's part of a group called the Phoenix Five, power brokers of the first order. Anyone with either business or political aspirations would do well to genuflect and kiss their rings. Plus, Kenly and his wife are big in the charity scene. No newspaper is going to take on Rantwist when he's got a heavyweight like that in his corner, without some seriously credible evidence to back it up."

I sighed. From the start, going after Rantwist had felt like an uphill battle. That hill was looking more and more like the face of a cliff.

"None of these cases has reached the plea stage, so there's still a chance the public defender's office will pick up on them and blow the whistle," I said hopefully.

In response to Macy's raised eyebrow, I explained. "The public defenders rarely have time to look at a file until the date scheduled for the pretrial conference, which is the day set by the court for the prosecutor and the defense attorney to get together and agree on whether to go to trial or work out a plea agreement. If they work out a plea agreement, the defendant pleads guilty to whatever was agreed to, and there's no trial. I still hope the public defender's office will figure things out at the pretrial conference and handle the whistle blowing on their own. I'm not saying I have a lot of hope, based upon what everyone I've talked to has said about how the system works, but maybe we should at least give them a chance."

"So you're gonna wait until some poor schmuck gets screwed, and then you out the county attorney?" Macy asked with narrowed eyes.

"If we do our homework, if it gets that far the poor schmuck will have his plea overturned."

Macy and Cal nodded. The nodding went on a bit longer than necessary.

"Maybe we should call it a night," I said. "I still have to give Ralph a bath, and I have a file I need to review for tomorrow."

Macy roused herself. "I got stuff to do too. I got a bunch of dirty support hose, and they ain't gonna wash themselves." Then, looking at Cal coquettishly, she added, "I could use an escort home, though."

Cal, who was close to falling asleep, rolled his head to look at her. "You live next door. I'm the one who needs an escort. I live on the goddamn second floor."

Macy looked as though she was about to hurl a not-so-polite rejoinder at him. Then her eyes lit up. Clearly she perceived an opportunity to get to know Cal better.

"No problem. I'll help you to your condo. Kate, you don't mind if I leave this stuff here, do you?" Macy asked, gesturing at the drink cart and snacks and nearly falling off the couch in the process.

"No problem at all," I said graciously.

I watched the two leave my condo with their arms around each other, probably more for support than out of affection. I wondered if I should follow them to make sure they made it safely to Cal's condo. Once they got there, I was pretty sure I wouldn't have to worry about escorting Macy back to her place. I decided against following them to Cal's, because it seemed like it would be a real romance killer if I did.

I heard Ralph reposition himself in the foyer and sigh. I figured I'd better give him his bath and lift his pariah status. I closed the door behind Macy and Cal and looked over at him.

"C'mon, boy. Bath time."

Ralph did not have an extensive vocabulary, but he did know what the word bath meant. For the most part he is a strong, loyal, well-behaved beast, but when it comes to baths, all bets are off. He hates them.

Before I could grab him by the collar, he bolted to the couch and tried to crawl under it. Unfortunately, there was only a six-inch clearance under the couch, and Ralph needed much, much more than that. I'd give him high marks for trying, though. After a spate of frantic pushing, shoving, and scratching, Ralph ended up with his butt on one side of the couch and his head on the other, with the couch teetering dangerously on his back.

I went over to Macy's drink cart and made myself a gin and tonic, and then somehow managed to get Ralph out from under the couch with minimal damage to him, me, the couch, and my drink. I dragged him into my bedroom and shut the door. I knew from experience that the only way I could get Ralph into the tub was to go in with him. I changed into a one-piece bathing suit I'd purchased at a discount store for just this purpose. The suit was a nauseating shade of yellow-green and was a size too small, so I gave myself a wedgie every time I bent over. But I wasn't about to waste a good bathing suit on Ralph's bath time. I grabbed some shampoo and filled the tub about halfway. Ralph was smashed up against the bedroom door, willing with all his might for it to open.

I tried a sweet-voiced appeal first.

"Come on, Ralphy, come on, boy," I said merrily as I put one foot in the tub and swirled it around in the water.

"Ohhhh, this is so much fun," I gushed with feigned ecstasy.

Ralph was not buying it.

I removed my foot from the tub and went to Plan Two, which entailed grabbing Ralph by the collar, dragging him across the floor, and shoving him into the tub. This process, though eventually effective, took about fifteen minutes of intense physical activity accompanied by creative and extensive cursing.

Once Ralph and I were finally in the tub, I dolloped shampoo on him and lathered him up. Then I rinsed him off, after which he leaped out of the tub and shook himself, as the result of which my bathroom acquired a "post-Katrina" look. I took a shower and washed off the wet dog hair plastered to every surface and crevice of my body, not bothering to remove my bathing suit.

After I got out I threw a pair of shorts on over my suit, put on my tennis shoes, and took Ralph outside for a walk. His coat was completely dry after a few minutes in the Phoenix heat. It was still fairly early in the evening, so I decided to take him on a longer walk than usual.

I heard sirens as we turned the corner at the end of the block. Police cars came from all directions and screeched to a halt in front of an office building about a block away. Ralph and I stopped to watch. Suddenly a figure emerged out of the shadows of an apartment building to the left of us. I tried to pull

Ralph out of the way, but the figure, now identifiable as a rather large, blond woman wearing high heels, stumbled over Ralph's flank and came crashing down.

"Sonofabitch," she exclaimed in a voice that was somewhat low for a woman's. After glancing at Ralph and me, she said, "Sorry."

Within seconds she was back on her feet. She bolted across the street, dodging the heavy mall traffic, and disappeared into the darkness.

I was pretty sure we had just run into (literally) the Paris Hilton Bandit. Whoever she was, she was wearing really great shoes.

A few seconds later a man wearing a deputy sheriff's uniform trotted down the sidewalk toward us.

"Did you see anyone running away from that office building over there?" he asked, pointing to the building where a dozen or so parked police cars lit the street with red and white strobe lights.

The officer's voice sounded vaguely familiar. I took a closer look at his face, which was partially obscured by the brim of a baseball cap bearing the insignia of the sheriff's department. It was Bryan Turner.

I pointed toward the mall parking lot and said, "She went thataway."

Bryan shouted something into his walkie-talkie, and some of the police cars took off toward the mall.

"Wait a minute," he said. "You're Kate, Kate Williams, right?"

I considered denying it. I was not dressed for the occasion, or any other occasion for that matter. I had not bothered to put on makeup or comb, much less style, my hair. My yellow-green bathing suit glowed iridescently, and my cutoffs had followed the lead of my bathing suit so that I now had a double wedgie. Ralph, on the other hand, looked quite nice with his freshly cleaned hair puffing out softly around him.

I reluctantly decided to tell Bryan the truth, since it was likely he'd need a witness statement from me, and I didn't want to lie in a sworn statement.

I pretended first to study Bryan, and then assume a look of sudden recognition.

"Why, Bryan. What a surprise. What are you doing out here?" Dumb question. He was in uniform, with a load of police and sheriff's department personnel, and cop cars behind him. What did I *think* he was doing? Making a pizza run?

"I heard on my radio that a burglary was in progress, so I headed over." He was nice enough to explain the obvious without a hint of sarcasm. We both knew it was a stupid question, though.

"I mean, I thought you were solely a desk jockey," I said, trying to save face. Whatever face saving I'd accomplished was undone, though, because then I hiccupped. Not a soft, ladylike hiccup, but a loud, movie-western, let's-have-another-round-of-whiskey hiccup.

"Nope. I'm the real deal," Bryan said, stifling a smile. "Look, I don't need to keep you standing here on the street. Would you mind giving me your address and telephone number? I or one of my guys can get a short statement from you later tonight."

I gave him my contact information, fluttered my fingers in a little wave, and turned in the opposite direction so I could beat a hasty retreat. I tried to make Ralph walk behind me to cover up my pants-in-butt-crack problem. However, Ralph, who had never before in his life heeled properly, walked at my side like a well-trained show dog.

As soon as we got back to the condo, I took off my shorts and bathing suit, put on my most flattering pair of jeans and a low-cut top, combed my hair into a ponytail, and threw on some lipstick. Then I washed the glasses Cal, Macy, and I had used and stashed the drinks cart and its contents in the closet. If Bryan showed up later on to take my statement, I wanted to undo the impression I must have just made.

I remembered that I still hadn't looked at the file MJ had given me earlier, so I retrieved it from my briefcase and sat down to read while I waited for Bryan or someone else from the sheriff's department to call or come by. I was soon absorbed in the file's contents.

The defendant, Greg Janner, was stopped for speeding at 2 a.m. on July first. The officer making the stop noticed several boxes in the backseat of the car, one of which was open. Baggies filled with a white substance were visible inside the box. The officer called for backup, and a drug-sniffing dog was brought out to the scene by the canine unit. The dog confirmed that the baggies were filled with some sort of drug, and judging by the intensity of the dog's reaction, it was pretty good stuff. Janner was arrested and held on suspicion of possession of drugs for the purpose of sale, and the next day the police lab confirmed that the white stuff in the baggies was indeed a particularly potent form of cocaine. The total street value of the cocaine found in Janner's car was estimated to be around two million dollars.

It seemed pretty cut-and-dried to me, but the charging division of the county attorney's office reduced the charge to misdemeanor possession. An unsigned file note merely read "Evidentiary problems require lesser charge." I didn't notice any evidentiary problems in the file, however. I re-read the arrest report. Clearly the officer had probable cause to stop Janner's vehicle since it was clocked going seventy miles per hour in a thirty-five-mile-per-hour zone. Since the drugs were in plain view in the backseat, the officer did not need a warrant to search the car.

The only other possibility was that there was a defect in the drug evidence's chain of custody not reflected in the file. In criminal cases, the law enforcement authorities must record how the evidence is handled from the time it is taken by law enforcement personnel until it is produced in court. This procedure is necessary to counter claims by the defendant's counsel that the evidence was tampered with and is therefore inadmissible at trial.

If there was a chain-of-custody issue, the relevant reports would be in the sheriff's office.

The phone rang, startling me. I picked up the receiver and said, "Kate Williams," using my office voice.

A youthful voice responded. "Miss Williams, this is Deputy Sheriff Bretzky. Chief Turner asked me to call you and ask if we could schedule your interview for tomorrow afternoon."

I felt a stab of disappointment. I was secretly hoping Bryan would come by my apartment tonight, giving me a chance to rehabilitate myself before the image of me earlier this evening was permanently burned into his memory. But not only was Bryan not coming over, it seemed as though he'd passed me off to a subordinate.

"That's not a problem, Deputy," I said, but did not mean. "Can you tell me where and when I will be interviewed?"

"Deputy Turner said he could drop by your office about one tomorrow afternoon, and if you're okay with taking a late lunch, he could get your statement over hamburgers at Mabel's."

Mabel's was a small café downtown that catered to a more upscale crowd: one willing to pay twelve dollars plus for a hamburger. Far from being fobbed off, now I'd been invited to lunch with Turner. It sounded almost like a request for a date, with Deputy Bretzky playing Cyrano de Bergerac.

"That would be fine, Deputy," I said, trying not to sound as pleased as I felt.

A wave of exhaustion hit me after I hung up, and with good reason. Alcohol, excitement, and exercise are not a good combination. I headed to bed, not bothering to change into a nightgown or wash my face. Ralph was already conked out on the left side of the bed. In past evenings I had made it very clear to Ralph that I preferred the right side. After all, I have some limits.

Chapter Twelve

I woke up late. I wasn't too concerned, though. I figured after everything that had happened the day before, I deserved a little extra sleep. I was not about to rush to get ready for work, either. I would be late, and everyone would just have to accept it. Alan would have to wait a little longer to start spying on me.

After I walked Ralph, I made coffee and settled in with the newspaper. I wanted to see if there was anything about last night's events.

Sure enough, there was an article on the front page headlined "Paris Hilton Bandit Strikes Again." According to the article, a woman had tried to burglarize the offices of Albert Kenly, the man Cal described the night before as one of Rantwist's major political backers. The burglar's activities were interrupted by the night guard, who described the thief as a tall blond with "killer legs." The burglar decked the night guard with a left hook and took off running. Another witness (me) said the suspect ran into the mall parking lot. The responding officers were unable to find her after an extensive search of the mall premises. The burglar had managed to break into a locked file cabinet in Kenly's office, but, according to Kenly, nothing of value was taken. The public was warned to be on the lookout for anyone acting suspiciously.

I remembered Cal mentioning that Albert Kenly was extremely well-to-do. His offices had to be loaded with expensive technology. I wondered why the burglar hadn't tried to take some of it. Maybe she thought the file cabinet, since it was locked, had money in it. If that was the case, she wasn't the type of grab-and-run thief I was used to defending in Chicago. She had a lot of moxie to stick around for the time it took to break into a locked file.

After Ralph and I each polished off a couple bowls of Trix, I wandered off to my bedroom to get ready for work.

I called Macy before I left. She didn't answer her phone, and I wasn't surprised. She was probably still in bed sleeping off a hangover.

I left the drink cart in front of her door and took the elevator to the garage. An unfamiliar dark-blue SUV was parked next to mine with the engine running. I couldn't see through its tinted windows, so I couldn't tell who, if anybody, was inside.

Someone was inside as it turns out, because the dark-blue SUV pulled out after I did and followed me into the traffic. It stuck behind me all the way to work, and pulled into a parking space about three cars down from mine. I was thoroughly miffed by this point. I got out of my car and headed toward the unfamiliar vehicle. The driver got out as I approached. It was Alan. He was really taking his assignment seriously.

"You're late," he said.

"Hello to you, too," I said. "Why the hell were you in the garage of my building, and why the hell did you follow me to work?"

"Rantwist told me to keep track of you. You were there when he said it. So I'm keeping track of you."

That damned smirk again.

"You're insane," I said earnestly, as though I would be able to convince him. "Rantwist meant for you to oversee my work, not my life. If I catch you anywhere near me outside work, I'll file a complaint against you for harassment."

I tried to wheel around and stomp off, but my heel caught in a seam in the concrete floor, so my body turned but my foot stayed put. I pulled at the heel, but it wouldn't budge. After a few hard jerks, it finally came free. I marched away, but the dramatic effect was greatly diminished.

"How in God's name did that burglar run in six-inch heels last night, when I can't even walk in heels half that height?" I grumbled under my breath.

I got to my office with every intention of settling in and getting some work done before my ten o'clock court appearance, only to find Sam standing on my desk staring intently at the light fixture.

"Are you replacing a bulb?" I asked reasonably.

Sam shushed me furiously. "Checking for bugs," he whispered.

"You really are a cleanliness fanatic," I whispered back.

"Not that kind of bug." Sam triumphantly held up a small metal disc. He placed it on my desk and motioned for me to go out into the hallway, then jumped off the desk and followed me, closing my office door once we were outside.

"This can't be happening," I said with dismay. "Who would place a transmitter in my office?"

"Alan," said Sam without hesitation.

I knew he was right. Bugging my office was completely consistent behavior for a man who lay in wait in my garage, then followed me to work.

"Give me that bug. I'm going to shove it up his nose," I said angrily. I'd had it with Alan and his super-spy tactics.

"He'll just plant another, and that one will be harder to find," Sam said calmly.

He made sense. Too bad, because I really wanted to shove that thing up Alan's nose.

"I'll put it someplace where it will pick up enough sound to keep Alan occupied, but won't do you any harm," Sam continued.

"Where?" I asked.

"Underneath the urinal in the men's bathroom."

I looked at Sam in admiration. "Good idea."

Sam went into my office and returned carrying a roll of tape and the transmitter.

"Come back for another visit when you're through 'taping,'" I whispered, hoping Sam appreciated the double meaning. I didn't think he did, though. He strode off without comment, carrying the transmitter like it was a dead mouse, probably because he knew that at some point Alan must have touched it.

I went into my newly debugged office and called MJ. When she answered, I told her she could come to my office and pick up the Janner file. Of course, I didn't call it the Janner file, but referred to it simply as The File. I was developing a healthy sense of paranoia and was afraid the phone might be tapped.

MJ trotted in moments later, and I handed her the file, which she placed inside a folder labeled "cake recipes." In response to my questioning look, she said, "In case anyone stops me, they won't get suspicious."

I looked at her doubtfully. "A file marked 'cake recipes' isn't suspicious?"

"Nope. Beth's got one for cookie recipes she's always lending out, Jenny's got one for hairdo ideas, and Sam's got one for magazine clippings of Brad Pitt."

I made a mental note to ask Beth about her cookie recipes.

Sam returned just as MJ was leaving. They air-kissed each other in passing.

Sam drew himself up and saluted. "Mission accomplished. Even as we speak Alan is listening to the dulcet sound of Dan Siever pissing."

I smiled. "It really is getting awfully cloak-and-dagger around here," I commented. Then I told him about Alan following me to work.

"He really is a piece of work," Sam said when I was finished. "This is a new low, even for him. He usually confines his spying activities to the office."

"Do you think Rantwist asked him to expand the scope of the surveillance?"

"Could be, but more likely it's because Alan's got the hots for you, so he's using his assignment as an excuse to stalk you."

I was genuinely horrified, and my face must have shown it, because Sam hurriedly added, "But don't worry. Alan gets a crush on every new woman employee. I guess hope springs eternal, or maybe he's just never taken a good look at himself in the mirror or sniffed his own armpit. After you shut him down a hundred times or so, he'll get the point."

"If that was meant to make me feel better, it didn't work," I said glumly.

Sam wisely changed the subject. "Did the file MJ smuggled out of Misdemeanors have anything interesting in it?"

I told Sam about the Janner file and my plan to question Bryan Turner about it at lunch today.

Sam raised one eyebrow. "Lunch? I'm jealous," he said.

"Don't be. I'm going to lunch with Turner so he can take my statement. I witnessed a burglar's getaway last night."

Sam looked at me in silence and then said "Your life is way too complex."

I nodded sadly. He was right on the mark. I'd moved to Phoenix to simplify my life, but here I was heading up an investigation of my own boss and, as of last night, was a witness in a burglary case.

I must have done something really nasty in the past that brought on some seriously negative karma. Maybe it was the time I glued my college roommate's lips together because I couldn't take any more of her perky morning personality. (She habitually jumped out of bed at 6 a.m. and heralded each new day with song. I, on the other hand, was not now nor had I ever been a morning person. I needed several cups of coffee before being capable of civilized behavior. From my point of view, she deserved what she got.)

Also, there was the time I locked my ex–law partner, Randall, into a janitor's closet and left him there overnight. Like my college roommate, he'd brought it on himself: I was in the midst of a truly heinous PMS episode, and he told me I should lose weight because I was looking a little pudgy.

Fortunately Sam interrupted my mental rambling before I'd gone too far down memory lane. "Are you going to ask Bryan about the chain of custody issue?" he asked.

"I intend to get into it as soon as we finish my statement, which shouldn't take long because all I saw was a woman running away from the scene of the crime. Since it was dark, I didn't get a good look at her face."

"Is this the attempted burglary that was in the newspaper this morning?"

I nodded.

"Was she really running in six-inch heels?"

I nodded again.

"That's impressive. I can barely manage *walking* in *three*-inch heels," said Sam with feeling.

I did not ask him if and when he wore women's high-heeled shoes. I sincerely did not want to know.

"I'd better head over to court. I've got a ten o'clock motion hearing in front of Judge Schwartz," I said

"Oh gawd. Judge Schwartz?"

"Yes. Is there something I should know about him?"

"He's an asshole," intoned Sam with feeling.

"I'm used to difficult judges. I'll survive."

"Well, good luck. I'm warning you though; Schwartz is a whole new level of asshole."

Sam promised he would check the transmitter from time to time to make sure it was still on the urinal, saluted again, and then left.

I glanced at the clock and saw that I had a little less than fifteen minutes to walk to court. I grabbed the file and took off. The case, a hit-and-run, was straightforward, and the charge of manslaughter was consistent with the facts. The defense attorney had filed a motion to exclude certain evidence from the trial, but it seemed to have little or no basis. At least I had one case I could take on without questioning the severity of the charge. I guessed a private attorney was representing the defendant. I checked the status sheet on the inside of the file front. I was right.

I arrived at the courthouse perspiring. I found the courtroom and checked the docket posted outside the door. My motion was up next.

I went in and walked to the prosecutor's table just as the bailiff announced the judge's entrance. I stood until the judge was seated, then sat down and opened my file.

"Mrs. Williams?" he asked in an irritatingly high voice; kind of like Truman Capote without the lisp.

I stood again. "Yes, your honor, and if you please, I prefer being addressed as Ms."

"Mrs. Williams, in this court attorneys do not sit unless and until I say they may. I'm not going to hold you in contempt only because I understand you are new at the prosecutor's office."

This guy would get along great with Alan and his Rules of Protocol, I thought.

I nodded obediently and let the Mrs. thing pass.

"Now let's try this again the right way," he said. He trotted down the two steps from the judge's bench, holding his robes waist high as if he were walking in floodwaters, and disappeared through the door to his chambers.

I kept my eyes on defense counsel, an attorney named Brock Babitch, since he seemed to know Schwartz' rules or at least hadn't been caught breaking any yet.

Brock stood at alert, eyes forward, so I did the same. I heard the judge turn the doorknob, and suddenly Brock sat down. Nanoseconds later, when the judge entered the courtroom, he stood up deferentially.

"Wrong, Mrs. Williams. Wrong, wrong, wrong," screeched Schwartz. "You must stand up *when* I enter. You were standing *before* I entered and just continued to stand."

I heard Babitch snicker. I made a mental note to add him to my People to Get Back At list.

"Again! We have to do this again!" Schwartz turned, his robe swirling dramatically around him, and went back into his chambers.

Brock and I sat down and watched the door apprehensively. The tension was palpable.

The knob turned and we both jumped up, timing it perfectly so Schwartz could see us stand as he entered.

I thought, *This is why I went to law school? To play Simon Says?*

Having not been given permission to sit, we continued to stand.

"Mr. Babitch. This is your motion. You proceed first," said the judge.

"If the court pleases, I have a short reply to the response filed by Mrs. Williams. May I approach the bench?"

Schwartz nodded. Babitch handed me a copy of his reply then went to hand the judge another copy. In doing so he leaned against the podium. Judge Schwartz lunged and hit Brock on the shoulder with his gavel.

"Never, never, never touch the court's bench," he screamed. Babitch rapidly retreated, massaging his injured shoulder.

Since he faked me out on the standing/sitting thing, I had no sympathy for him.

Brock and I presented our arguments to the court, flinching whenever Schwartz moved, and Schwartz took the ruling under advisement, which I thought was ridiculous since the defense clearly had no basis for their motion. But then the whole situation had been ridiculous. Sam said Schwartz was mean. He didn't mention he was a psycho.

I saw the ubiquitous Alan sitting in the back of the courtroom as I left. I was no longer the least bit surprised to see him.

On my way back to the office I stopped off at Cuties Sub Shop for a cold can of diet coke and a cookie, and said hi to Mitchie, who was working behind the counter again. He seemed a lot calmer today, but still glanced nervously at the door. I told him "MJ's not with me today, but I'll say hi to her for you when I see her later." His face relaxed into a slight smile. "Better you than me," he said ruefully.

I figured he and MJ had another fight, but was not about to ask. No way did I want to get involved in their personal issues.

I still had an hour before my lunch appointment with Bryan, so I reviewed a few more cases after I got back. I was putting my notes in a file when Bryan knocked on my open door and asked if I was ready to go to lunch. I found his habit of knocking absolutely charming. Forget flowers and candy. All I wanted was a man who knocked before entering. I had really lowered the bar since moving to Phoenix.

Bryan said we would take his car, because even though the restaurant was not far, it was too hot outside to walk.

I let out a small gasp when we got to his car. It was the SUV Alan was driving this morning.

"Did you lend Alan your car today?" I asked. "I saw him driving this car or one exactly like it earlier."

"This is a county vehicle. Anyone who works for the county can use it, provided it's for official business. So it's very possible that Alan drove it this morning."

Apparently Alan thought stalking me was "official business."

Bryan politely held the door open for me, but I hesitated before climbing in. My inner child was afraid of getting Alan-cooties. I reasoned with my inner child that he hadn't sat in the passenger's seat, so only the driver's side had cooties. My inner child bought this reasoning, and I got into the car.

I had second thoughts as soon as I was inside the van. I could smell Alan's scent, a combination of old sweat and food. I sat on something crackly. The edge of a piece of paper was wedged in the seat. I retrieved it and I recognized it as a penciled layout of my condo, with details right down to the location of Ralph's bowl.

I decided not to mention anything about it to Bryan. The whole thing was just too creepy. I shoved the diagram in my pocket just as he slid into the driver's seat. "Buckle up," he said. "It's the law."

I dutifully did so and then noticed that Bryan had not secured his own.

"*You* buckle up, or I'll make a citizen's arrest," I said teasingly.

"Sorry," he said as he fastened his seat belt. "It's pretty adolescent, I know, but I just can't get over the feeling that it's so uncool."

We chatted about the weather and other neutral topics during the short ride to the restaurant. He valet-parked the car, which I thought was very classy, and we headed inside.

The maître d' greeted Bryan like an old friend, then led us to a private booth in the back of the restaurant. The booth was set into the wall, and an opaque curtain covered the entrance. I felt like I was at a meeting of the Cosa Nostra.

After we were seated, I commented, "You must come here fairly often. The maître d' seems to know you quite well."

Bryan smiled, and said "This is the only restaurant in the area with a suitably remote booth. It comes in handy when you're discussing things you don't want anyone to overhear."

"Is this where you take most of your dates, then?" The words were out before I could exercise reason and voluntary motor skills to keep my mouth shut. There were times when I was convinced I was possessed by a spirit which normally hung out in Geraldo Rivera's body but inhabited mine once in a while just for a change of scenery.

If Bryan was put off by my dumb, none-of-your-business question, he did not show it.

"Actually, I bring very few dates here. There are places far more private than this, and less expensive, too, unless you order room service. I usually limit my visits here to when the county will pick up the tab."

His tone, which had been light and a bit teasing, turned serious. "I don't want *anyone* to overhear our discussion," he repeated.

I had to laugh. I couldn't help it. Bryan's tone was so dramatic. But I mean really; a booth with curtains that didn't quite meet in the middle was hardly high security. An image popped into my head of us sitting under the "cone of silence" used by the agents of C.O.N.T.R.O.L. in Get Smart, a TV show from the '60s still shown in reruns. The cone of silence was completely ineffective, because the agents inside the cone couldn't hear each other, while people on the outside could hear them perfectly.

Bryan didn't seem to see the humor in the situation. "I heard Sam found a bug in your office this morning," he said. "I have a suspicion Alan may have planted it."

I no longer felt like laughing.

"Why do you think that?" I asked.

"Because Alan is a paranoid son of a bitch and considers any new attorney with your experience and intelligence to be a threat to his position. Plus, I stopped by his office before I picked you up today. His door was open, so I looked in and saw him crouched over what looked like a wireless receiver. I could hear voices coming out of the receiver, but I couldn't understand what they were saying. It sounded as if running water was interfering with the sound quality of the transmission. Anyway, Alan was taking notes on a legal pad, and at the top of the legal pad he'd written the letters 'KM.' He didn't notice me watching, so I left without saying anything. I ran into Sam as I was coming to your office, and I told him what I'd just seen. I asked if there was an internal investigation going on. He told me about finding the bug in your office and removing it to the men's room. By the way, is Sam always so nervous? He was stuttering and blushing all the time we were talking."

It didn't take much for Sam to spill to Bryan everything he knew about the bug. I made a mental note to tell Sam to avoid talking about our situation to men with pretty faces, because he got verbal diarrhea around them.

I gave Bryan a blank stare, or at least what I hoped looked like a blank stare. "My goodness." I said in feigned confusion. "I'm sure what you're saying about Alan can't be true." I did not address Bryan's question concerning Sam's demeanor. What could I say? *Sam stuttered and blushed because he thinks you're hot?*

"Trust me," said Bryan darkly. "Alan is capable of being a real jerk. I know this from personal experience."

I looked at him questioningly, but he did not elucidate. Instead, he abruptly changed the subject.

"Do you know what you want to order?" he asked.

I nodded, and he opened the curtain and signaled the waiter to come over. We both ordered mushroom-and-Swiss burgers with fries.

After the waiter left, Bryan pulled out a piece of paper from the file he'd brought along. "We should be able to finish your statement before the food comes," he said. "I doubt there is much you can add to what you already said last night."

I dutifully repeated what I had said the night before and then added more detail in response to Bryan's in-depth questioning. The only new information I could provide was that, unlike the other witnesses, I was able to describe the style and identify the brand name of the shoes the burglar was wearing.

When I got to the part where she tripped over Ralph, Bryan interrupted. "Did she say anything when she tripped, or anytime for that matter?"

I nodded. "When she tripped."

"What did her voice sound like?"

I gave it some thought before answering. "Low for a woman's. But very polite, under the circumstances."

Bryan leaned toward me. What I'd just said seemed to pique his interest.

"What do you mean when you say her voice was 'low for a woman's'?"

"I mean just that. Her voice was low for a woman's voice."

"Could it have been high for a man's voice?" he asked.

I realized what he was getting at. "You think the 'she' might be a 'he'?"

"What I think doesn't matter. You're the witness here. What do you think?"

"Well, if she was a man, that might explain her height. She looked to be well over six feet tall. Plus, she had pretty broad shoulders for a woman, and those Chanel shoes must have been at least a size ten. I didn't even know they made them that big." I paused and thought it over some more. "But if she was a he, he had a hell of a lot of practice walking—no, *running* in six-inch heels. Maybe he's a transvestite runway model. That would certainly narrow the field of search."

Bryan laughed. "I don't know about that. I hear the Phoenix police's detective division has quite a few of them."

I smiled in appreciation of the inside joke. I knew the Phoenix police department and the sheriff's department had a long-standing rivalry, sort of like the army and the marines.

The waiter interrupted us to deliver our hamburgers. I took a huge bite out of mine, so my next question was a bit muffled. "Is there something else your guys found that makes you think she might be a he?"

Bryan nodded. " The burglar tossed a half-full can of Diet Coke on the floor just before she ran out of the office building. The can opening tested positive for saliva, but a preliminary DNA check showed male DNA only."

"Wow," I commented. "DNA tests are not cheap. And you got some results overnight. Since when do you guys pull out all the stops on a mere attempted burglary?"

Bryan grimaced. "Since the victim of the attempted burglary donated *big* to both the sheriff's campaign and the county attorney's campaign, that's when."

"You are referring to Mr. Kenly, I presume?" I was pleased to see the surprise on Bryan's face when I pulled that one out of my hat. "I read the paper before I left for work," I said.

"In our defense, though," continued Bryan, "we're not just playing favorites with crime victims. The description you and our other witnesses gave of the burglar matches that of a suspect in a robbery last week."

"The Paris Hilton Bandit," I said.

"You do read the paper a lot."

I wasn't sure I liked his inference that I had nothing to do besides read the newspaper. Admittedly, when it came to my social life, this was largely true, but I wasn't one of those attorneys who sat at her desk and read the newspaper all day.

He must have picked up on my dismay. "I don't mean that reading the paper is *all* you do. You've already got a reputation around here as a hard worker," he said apologetically.

I doubted that I could be considered a hard worker at the rate I was going. I was spending more time investigating my boss than handling my caseload, but then maybe the bar for high achievers in the county attorney's office was a lot lower than in private practice. Anyway, it was a nice thing for Bryan to say.

Then I remembered I was here to talk to him about something other than burglary of Kenly's office.

"Do you know anything about a drug bust involving a guy named Janner?" I asked. I'd found in my practice that a quick change of subject threw people off balance, and they often tended to be more truthful as a result.

Bryan looked taken aback. "Why?" he asked. "Are you working on that case?"

"No," I said. I looked at Bryan carefully to gauge his next reaction. "It was assigned to the misdemeanor division."

"*What?*" Bryan's surprise seemed genuine enough. "No way. That was a huge bust. One of the biggest we've made this year. It must have gone to Misdemeanors by mistake."

"I don't think so," I said. "At least according to the charge in the file."

"No fucking way," Bryan blurted out angrily. Mr. Polite-and-in-control had disappeared and been replaced by an emotionally charged, obscenity-spewing cop. I had no doubt that his reaction was genuine.

I told him about the comment in the file that evidentiary problems prevented a higher charge of felony possession for sale.

"No fucking way," Bryan repeated. "I know that case. I helped process the evidence after the initial call for backup. We did everything by the book. The chain-of-custody record is attached to each of the boxes of evidence, and there should be another copy of it in the case file."

"There wasn't a copy in the file. I looked. So where's the evidence kept?" I asked.

"Where drugs are involved, it's kept in the safe in the evidence room at the sheriff's department. No one has access to that safe except the county attorney, the sheriff, and me."

I smiled at him sweetly.

"No," he said.

"Why not?" I asked, innocence itself. "If you've got the code or whatever it is you need to get into the safe, why don't we just go check and see if there's a problem with the evidence or the chain-of-custody report?"

"First, there's no 'we.' You are not authorized to go into the evidence room at all unless you have written permission from the county attorney. Second, even though I'm authorized to go in, I have to sign in with the guard and specify which boxes of evidence I want to see and why. Then I need to sign and date the chain-of-custody records attached to the boxes. Those records become part of the evidence, so if something is missing or out of order, I'm the first one they'll suspect because I have absolutely no reason to look at the evidence at this point."

"Yes you do," I said. "I gave you the reason. You were in on a major drug arrest, and I just told you it was charged as a misdemeanor. You're only checking to find out why. The remarkable thing is that it's the truth, so you don't even have to make anything up."

"Uh-huh. So, acting upon knowledge gained from you, someone who has absolutely no connection with the case, and instead of talking to my supervisor about it, or going to the attorney in charge of the case, I take it upon myself to check the evidence, thereby leaving myself open to a charge of mishandling or, worse, stealing evidence if in fact something is missing even though the chain-of-custody record is clean. Then it becomes my word that I did not take the evidence against the world's more logical conclusion that I did. If I look at the Janner stuff, it's only going to be after I go through proper channels."

"But you don't need to go through all that. I would back you up," I protested, *and I'll cover your ass you wimp*.

"I appreciate that, but you're a lousy witness. Even if you could explain away the fact that you took a file home and reviewed it without authorization, you're in the same boat. Why didn't you just tell your supervisor? Why continue a clandestine operation if not for some nefarious reason?"

Clandestine? Nefarious? He reads way too many detective novels.

"Okay. Point taken, but let me tell you why I didn't, and won't, tell Rantwist about the Janner file, so we can take that issue off the table." I reminded him of our first conversation earlier in the week when I told him about the overcharged Larkin case. Bryan stared at me blankly. He obviously did not remember the Larkin case.

"The naked guy on Third and Central," I said.

"Oh, yeah. I remember now. I said I would check into it, didn't I? I'm sorry. I forgot." Since he had the decency to apologize and look ashamed, I passed up the opportunity to work the guilt angle.

I explained to Bryan how Rantwist had reacted when I asked him about the overcharge, how he later reprimanded me and ordered me to bring MJ back in line when he got word she was asking around about other undercharged misdemeanor files, and, as the final injustice, how he assigned Alan to the task of watching over me to make sure I kept in line, an assignment Alan had expanded to include stalking me during my off-duty hours. As proof I pulled out the diagram of my condo and told Bryan where I found it.

I concluded, "Rantwist and his little side kick are up to something."

Bryan took the diagram from me and appeared to study it. "He's even included a little hat on the floor."

"That's not a hat. That's Ralph's bowl. Alan is good at detail, but he's not the best artist in the world."

'Who's Ralph and why does he leave his bowl on the floor?"

"Ralph is my dog, and he has no thumbs."

I took the diagram from Bryan. He was taking far too much interest in it.

"Do you think the Sheriff knows what Rantwist is doing?" I asked.

Bryan turned serious again and shook his head slowly. " Sheriff Harmon and Rantwist have known each other a while and have pretty much the same political backers, but I can't believe he knows what's going on. The overcharging thing might be something he'd overlook, but no way would he stand for undercharging, especially on a drug arrest. He hates dealers."

"So tell him about the Janner case," I suggested, "and get some sort of expedited permission to check the evidence."

Bryan laughed ruefully. "I could keep you out of it and talk to the attorney assigned to the case in misdemeanors then file a request with the sheriff, but I can guarantee Hal will send a copy of the request to Rantwist since the matter involves his office. There's no way we can keep Rantwist out of the loop."

"So," I said, slapping my hand lightly on the table. "Looks like you'll need to do this without an authorization to cover your butt. When do you think you can get into the evidence room?"

Bryan stared thoughtfully for while. "I'll stop by the evidence room just before five this afternoon," he said resignedly. "Everybody's pretty focused on the clock about then, so I'll have a better chance of leaving the 'what and why' portions of the sign-in sheet blank.

By the way, I take umbrage with your comment about covering my butt."

I triumphantly popped my last french fry into my mouth. Through the space between the curtains I could see the waiter hovering nearby. Sensing his opportunity, he swooped in and commandeered our plates. He asked if we wanted dessert in a manner that clearly conveyed that he hoped we did not.

I looked at my watch. It was after three o'clock. The noon shift was over, and the waiter likely wanted to move on with his life.

I shook my head in response to Bryan's questioning look, and Bryan said, "No dessert, just the check, thanks."

The waiter produced the check in record time. Bryan paid, and we left.

Bryan dropped me off in front of the building to spare me the heat of the garage and then drove off to park the car.

I knew something was going on as soon as I reached my floor. Most, if not all, of the staff were standing in the hall talking excitedly. MJ broke away from what looked like an especially intense conversation with Beth and Jenny and ran up to me. She grabbed my arm and pulled me into my office.

"Did you see the paper?" she demanded breathlessly.

"Yes. I read it this morning," I said, trying to remember anything I saw that might give rise to this level of emotion.

"No, no. Did you read the noon edition of the *Bugle*?"

The *Bugle* is published in Scottsdale, a suburb of Phoenix, and is the only paper in the state with a noon edition.

She dashed into the hall and grabbed a copy from a startled secretary, then ran back in and thrust it into my hands.

"Front page. Look."

The headline read "County Attorney Takes Hard Line on Sex Offenders." The article that followed stated that Rantwist had imposed felony charges against several defendants arrested for what were normally considered minor violations. The article went on to describe the cases as involving "acts against nature." Only the Larkin case was mentioned by name. When asked about the charges, Rantwist was quoted as saying, "I take criminal acts like this very seriously. These are the sorts of crimes that undermine our civilization. The evildoers who commit them are like termites eating away at our value structure."

Picking up on the termite reference, the reporter nicknamed Rantwist the "Exterminator."

The paper had not contacted the public defender's office to get their take on the Exterminator's philosophy.

"Sheesh," I said. "The article almost makes Rantwist sound noble."

"No shit," said MJ. "Beth said the phone's been ringing off the hook with well-wishers. She told me she's making a list of the callers' names so her voodoo club can put a curse on them. I guess they only meet Fridays. Boy, Beth really hates Rantwist. Considering he's like the umpteen-millionth county attorney she's worked for, that's really saying something, because we've had some real pips. The guy before Rantwist used to sit under his desk to eat lunch. He said it was the only place he felt safe. He was a real pig, too, and Beth had to rake under his desk every few days to clean out the sandwich wrappers, apple cores, and potato chip bags."

I half-listened to MJ's digressions. I was too concerned about where the reporter from the *Bugle* got his information. I didn't think Macy would call the newspaper after she'd promised not to. A more likely possibility was that either Rantwist himself or someone acting at his instruction slipped the information to the reporter. Rantwist knew I was concerned about the overcharging issue. Maybe there were others who were concerned as well. Realizing he'd guessed wrong when he relied on the chilling effect of the office's bureaucracy to keep things quiet, he or one of his pals might have tipped off the newspaper, but only as to the overcharged cases. Hopefully he hadn't figured out we were onto the undercharged cases as well. He came across in the article as a crusader for the American system of values, instead of a nut who charged defendants with crimes not authorized by the law, and his conservative political base loved it. I doubted his supporters would love his stance on drug dealers.

I told MJ I needed to make some calls and said I would talk to her and Sam when I was through.

As soon as MJ left, I called Bryan. His secretary said he was out of the office, and she did not expect him to return until about four thirty. I left a message for him to call me as soon as he got in. Bryan probably already knew about the article in the *Bugle*, since it was likely a big topic of conversation in his office as well, and I wanted to make sure he hadn't changed his mind about looking at the Janner evidence. I didn't see why the article would influence him one way or the other, but in light of his obvious hesitance to get involved in the whole mess, he might use the article as an excuse to delay things and see what else shook out as the result of any follow-up inquiries by the press.

Alan slithered into my office as I was hanging up the phone. He closed the door softly behind him and cleared his throat.

"Yes, Alan. I see you. What do you want?" I snapped.

"Did you read the article in the Scottsdale *Bugle* about the County Attorney?"

I nodded curtly and said, "Yes. Everyone in the building has."

"Then you may know that one of your cases, the Larkin case, was mentioned in the article. The County Attorney wanted me to forewarn you that you are likely to get calls from the media about the matter. He requests that you forward all such calls to him for a response so that the office's position remains consistent."

Because he's afraid I won't keep to the party line, I thought.

"In the event the media representatives place you in a position where you are either unable or it is extremely awkward for you to direct them to the County Attorney for a response, I have taken the liberty of preparing a statement for you."

Alan reached into the folder he was carrying, pulled out a sheet of paper, and handed it to me. I took it from him with the same two-fingered dead-mouse grip Sam had used earlier on the transmitter. The prepared statement read as follows:

I am the deputy county attorney to whom County Attorney Rantwist assigned the Larkin case. Mr. Rantwist has made prosecution of acts against nature a high priority of his administration. Mr. Rantwist wants to make Phoenix a better place to raise families, and we who work for him are honored to support him in this noble effort. We are in the front lines fighting alongside the County Attorney against the evil personified by men like Larkin.

I looked up from the paper at Alan

"I can't say this," I said.

"Why not?" demanded Alan.

"Well, for starters, I don't believe a word of it. Larkin does not represent evil. He represents a mixed-up guy who likes to expose his genitals to passersby. The only people who saw him were office workers stuck in rush-hour traffic who seemed to like the diversion. While I have no problem prosecuting Mr. Larkin to the full extent of the law, as I told Rantwist, I have *serious* reservations about prosecuting Larkin to the full extent *not* allowed by law."

Alan looked like he wanted to hit me, but he must have realized that if I quit or was fired, the county attorney would have no leverage to keep me in line.

"You refuse to cooperate, then?" He spat the words out.

"I refuse to lie," I spat back.

"Then I strongly suggest you stick to Plan A and refer all media to the County Attorney." He spoke slowly and with emphasis as he glared at me. He looked as though he wanted to add an "or else." I personally thought the additional verbiage would make for a nice dramatic effect, but he stopped short of saying it.

He turned to leave, then hesitated and swung around to face me again.

"I think you have a water leak in your office. Get it fixed."

It was all I could do not to laugh. My office did not have a leak, but there were lots of "leaks" in the men's room.

Sam strolled into my office not long after Alan left. He'd probably seen Alan come in and hid in the hallway until Alan left before going into my office, the big chicken.

"Why is your face so red?" he asked.

"Alan was just here, and I'm trying not to laugh," I choked.

"Yeah, that happens a lot around him," Sam said with a perfectly serious expression. "Say, would you mind if I left a little early today? I'm not going to get much done anyway with all the excitement here this afternoon."

"No problem. Tell me, though: how do you feel about all this? I mean the newspaper article," I asked.

Sam closed the door. "I feel like Rantwist's people planted that article to appeal to Rantwist's conservative supporters and put him in the best light. Rantwist and his cohorts knew you and maybe others in the office were questioning his charging policies, and they didn't want someone beating them to the newspapers."

"You're a good man, Sam," I said with feeling.

Sam blushed and fiddled with the knot in his tie. "No big deal. I noticed the article doesn't mention the undercharging on the Janner case, and I think there's a good chance Rantwist doesn't realize anyone is aware of it," he said quickly, seeming to rush his words to hide his embarrassment. "MJ did a good job of covering herself today. She knew Alan followed her into the misdemeanor division's file room when she went to return the Janner file. She shoved the file back into its slot while she was making a big show of filing the cake recipes. On her way back to her office, she told Jenny she'd put the recipes in the usual place, in case Jenny was looking for them. Thank God Jenny played along."

"What if he checked the file after MJ left? Wouldn't he get suspicious if he found an empty file labeled 'Cake Recipes' next to the Janner file?" I asked.

"MJ put a few recipes in the file just in case he looked in it."

"MJ bakes?" This was the most shocking news I'd heard all day.

"God, no. She told me she didn't have time to find any real recipes, so she made up a couple. Have you ever tried frosting with Bacos?"

"I don't think so, or at least I hope not," I said sincerely.

Sam and I smiled at one another.

"Except for the Bacos part, it sounds like MJ did a fine job," I said. "Hopefully no one will actually try out that recipe."

Sam glanced at his watch, and I remembered why he'd originally come by. "Go home, Sam. It's already four, though, so you're not getting much of a break."

Sam grinned. "It's better than nothing. At least I have a shot at beating the rush hour traffic."

Once Sam had left, I stared at the phone, willing it to ring. I hoped Bryan would take the same critical view Sam did about recent events.

CHAPTER THIRTEEN

I was still staring at the phone when I heard the five o'clock stampede to the elevator. I called Bryan's office again, but just got voice mail and a taped message suggesting somewhat condescendingly that I dial my party's direct extension if I knew it, and if I didn't know it, to stay on the line to access the office directory.

I hung up, hoping Bryan had simply decided to go straight to the evidence room from wherever he was instead of going back to his office first. Of course, I knew of a way to make sure that's what had happened. I could go over and hang around to see if Bryan made it there. I had never been to the evidence room, but based on what I knew about the set-up of the sheriff's department I thought I could find it.

I locked my office door and hurried toward the back stairs. It was still too close to five to try the elevator. The stairwell was surprisingly empty. Apparently it had not yet occurred to the hundreds of employees in the building that they could walk as well as ride to freedom.

Instead of exiting at the garage level, I walked two more levels down into the basement. I knew the basement ran under the garage and connected my office building with the building housing the sheriff's department. I had never taken this passage before, but Sam had mentioned it to me once, so I knew it existed.

I walked along the basement corridor until I came to a metal fence barrier manned by a young man in a deputy sheriff's uniform. I assumed this was the dividing line between the sheriff's territory and the county attorney's territory. The deputy looked especially pale in the fluorescent lighting. He was working on a crossword puzzle but looked up when he heard me approach.

I flashed my deputy county attorney's badge. He nodded and pointed to a sign-in sheet lying on the table next to him. I entered my name, relieved that he didn't ask me to state the purpose of my visit.

He opened the gate, and I passed through. After I had taken only a few steps down the corridor, though, he called out, "Wait!"

Damn, I thought. *Busted.*

"What's a four-letter word for 'oaf'?" he asked.

I stopped myself from reflexively answering *Alan.*

"Lout," I said.

"Perfect. That fits. Thanks a lot."

Yeah, and thanks a lot for nearly giving me a heart attack, I thought as I walked away.

My footsteps echoed in the empty hall. The guard at the gate was quickly out of sight as the hallway took a sharp jog first to the right, then to the left, and then meandered like the Mississippi River with the effect of doubling the distance from point A to point B. Whoever designed the basement layout had no concern for employees' feet. It seemed like I had been walking forever when I finally came to bank of elevators. An index on the wall beside them listed the various departments and the floors on which they were located. Neither the evidence room nor anything similar was listed. I checked the index again and noticed an area designated "Storage" located on the fifth floor next to the forensic lab. It seemed logical to me that the evidence room would be located next to the lab, so I decided to check out that area first.

No one was heading up to the office floors at this hour, so I had the elevator all to myself. When I got off on the fifth floor, there was a fairly substantial crowd waiting to go down, however. No one stopped or questioned me. Everyone was too busy jostling for a space on the elevator. I glanced back as the doors closed. The scene inside the elevator reminded me of a Hieronymus Bosch painting.

An arrow on the wall indicated the storage area was to the right, but I hesitated before heading in that direction. Now that I was here, I wasn't exactly sure what I was going to do. My original plan had been to find Bryan, but the floor was uncomfortably quiet after the departure of the employees. There was no sound except for the ubiquitous hum of the fluorescent lights.

I figured it would take Bryan about a half hour to locate and review the Janner evidence. So if he'd gone ahead with the plan, he should still be in the evidence room. There was still the possibility that the storage room and the evidence room were not one and the same, and Bryan was somewhere else in the building, but since I was already here, I might as well find the storage room and then wait outside fifteen minutes or so to see if he came out.

I walked quietly down the hall, stopping briefly to read each door sign. I turned the corner at the far end of the hall, but quickly pulled back. A guard was seated at a desk at the end of a short passageway. On the one hand, this was good news, because I was pretty sure now that the storage area was in fact the evidence room. On the other hand, I did *not* want the guard to see me, because I had no good explanation for why I was there. So I stayed put, listening carefully for anyone entering or leaving the evidence room.

I had been waiting about five minutes when I heard the guard get up and walk down the hall toward me. I opened the door of the room closest to me and stepped into pitch darkness inside. I heard the guard pause in the hall and speak with someone. Feeling my way around the room, I found a smaller metal door. I opened it and slipped inside. The door to the room opened, and bright lights came on, temporarily blinding me. Once my eyes adjusted, I looked around and saw that I had taken cover in a bathroom and was standing in one of the stalls.

I heard footsteps crossing the bathroom floor. The footsteps stopped outside my stall.

"Are you trying to relocate another one of Alan's bugs?" It was Bryan.

I opened the stall door. "I was looking for you," I said defensively. "I left a message for you to call me, and I didn't hear from you."

"So you decided to look for me in the men's room? What, you figure if I don't call you right back, it's because I've got better things to do in the men's room?"

It's hard to sound tough when you're blushing, but I gave it my best shot. "I wanted to see if you went to the evidence room. I was afraid you'd chicken out."

"Chicken out?" he asked incredulously. "You sound like you're talking about a high school dare. I said I would check things out, and I mean what I say."

"Like when you said you would check out the Larkin case," I said accusingly.

Once again he looked blank at the mention of Larkin. I rolled my eyes. "The naked guy on Third and Central."

"I didn't forget, I just haven't gotten around to it yet," he shot back. "You've got me too busy doing other things, like unauthorized visits to the evidence room."

I looked at him innocently. "I can't *make* you do anything. You did it of your own free will."

"You're pushy and self-righteous."

"You're a wimpy policy wank."

"What the hell is that supposed to mean?"

A noise coming from the hallway outside interrupted our schoolyard debate. We both looked nervously at the door. "We should get out of here," I whispered. "You may have a good reason to be in a men's room, but there is no way I can explain why I'm here."

Bryan nodded, and whispered back, "Wait for me at the basement level. I'll be down in a few minutes."

I gave him a questioning look.

"I did not come in here looking for you," he said, still whispering. "I just happened to see your shoes under the stall door. I came in here to use the men's room for the purpose for which is intended, although between your bathroom antics and Sam's, I'm not sure what that purpose is anymore."

In keeping with the maturity level of our conversation, I stuck my tongue out at him.

I eased the door open, checked to make sure the hallway was clear, and then scooted over to the elevator. I hit the down button with unnecessary force, as if that would bring a faster response, and waited impatiently.

"Hi there," said a voice behind me. "Working late?"

I forced myself to take a deep breath and stay calm. I turned around to face the guard. "Oh," I said in a timid voice. "I didn't know you were here. You frightened me." I was hoping this would explain why my legs were shaking.

"Sorry. This carpeting makes it hard to hear people coming up on you. Are you with the lab?"

I nodded. Honesty could take you just so far. I needed to refine my rule against lying to law enforcement personnel to account for emergency exceptions.

"Yeah, I just started," I said, flashing him a Miss America smile. "I'm still trying to figure things out."

"That must be why you're here so late. The M.O. for most people is to clear out no later than five. I don't know why they bother, though. They rush out of here and end up sitting in traffic. I've been on the three-to-midnight shift for about two years now, and it suits me just fine. I figure I save a couple hours of driving time each day."

With a ding, the elevator doors opened. I said good night to the guard and continued to grin insanely at him until they closed between us.

So much for post-9/11 security. All I'd run into tonight was a crossword-puzzle worker and a chatty night guard. The first didn't ask me any questions about why I was going to the sheriff's department after business hours, and the second didn't even bother to ask for identification.

I waited in the basement for nearly fifteen minutes until the elevator doors finally opened and Bryan emerged.

"What took you so long?" I blurted. Thinking better of it, I regrouped and said, "Forget it. You don't need to tell me."

"That's okay. I was not delayed by extensive and difficult bathroom duties. I was held up by a really lonely, talkative guard."

"Yeah," I nodded. "I caught some of that too."

"By the way, do you know you have toilet paper on your shoe?"

I looked down. Damn. He was right. No telling how long it had been there, but it would just have to stay put a little longer. I couldn't pin down its exact origin, so I was not about to pull it off with my fingers.

"Thanks for pointing that out," I said. "I will wear it with pride."

Then Bryan did something unexpected. He raised his hand and lightly brushed the hair out of my eyes.

"You're oddly endearing," he said.

"You're just odd," I shot back.

He let his hands drop to his sides and brusquely suggested we go to my office to discuss what he'd learned in the evidence room.

I immediately felt sorry for what I'd said but couldn't think of anything to say to remedy the situation. An apology was out of the question. Apologies were not my style. So I just nodded and charged off down the hallway toward the county attorney's building.

The same young guard sat at the midway point and, recognizing us, waved us on.

Bryan seemed tense and distracted, and he and I said nothing to each other during the trip to my office.

Attributing his silence to my previous remark, I thought he was being overly sensitive.

When we got to my office, Bryan had second thoughts. "Maybe we should go someplace else to talk. Alan may have figured out his transmitter was moved and rebugged the place."

"No problem," I said. "Just let me grab my purse."

At my suggestion, we agreed to meet at DeRoy's. Bryan had never been there before, so I gave him directions. He then escorted me to my parking space, checking my car and the surrounding area to make sure Alan the Stalker was off duty.

I was not far from DeRoy's when my cell phone rang. I answered, and Cal's basso voice boomed in my ear. "Where've you been?" he demanded. I guessed Cal had gotten my number from Macy. I'd given Macy my cell number and a copy of the key to my condo in case she needed to get hold of me for Ralph-related emergencies.

Oh my God—Ralph! I thought with alarm. I'd forgotten about him with all the excitement at my office.

"Oh, Cal! Is Ralph all right?" I asked worriedly.

"He's healthy as a horse. He shits like one too, by the way. I went and got him and took him for a walk after Macy called and said that you hadn't come home yet, and that Ralph was raising a racket in your condo."

"Thanks, Cal. I really appreciate it. I got caught up at work, and now I'm heading over to DeRoy's to meet with Bryan Turner."

"Don't," said Cal brusquely.

"Don't what?"

"Don't meet with Turner. Don't trust him. Don't trust anyone. I have something you need to see. Come to my condo ASAP. I'm in 206. I'll keep Ralph here with me. He's eaten everything in my refrigerator, but he's fine. Does he always whine until you put mustard on his meat?"

"Not all the time. Only when it's ham."

"It was ham."

"Listen, Cal, I won't take long with Turner, and there's nothing to worry about. DeRoy's is always packed at this hour. Nothing can happen with that many people around. I'll call you as soon as I leave to let you know I'm on my way."

I hung up before Cal could say anything more. I thought he was being a bit histrionic. He really needed to get a hobby.

I pulled into the parking lot at DeRoy's. What I'd told Cal was true: DeRoy's *was* packed at this hour. I had to circle the parking lot a few times until a spot opened up. I saw a county vehicle parked near the entrance, so I guessed Bryan was already inside.

I entered the smoke-filled restaurant and spotted him sitting in the bar area near the front. He was guarding an empty stool next to him. Based on the vulturine looks of the bystanders, empty seats were in big demand.

I slid onto the stool.

"Thank God you're here," he said. "Conspiracies to take the chair I saved for you abound."

"I'm surprised you were able to find anyplace at the bar to sit. Usually it's at least a twenty-minute wait for a table at this hour, so the patrons crowd the bar and order drinks to stave off starvation."

"I played the cop card," he said unashamedly.

"You flashed your badge? I'm surprised that worked. This is a pretty tough crowd."

"I told them I was with the no-smoking enforcement division."

"Is there a no-smoking enforcement division?"

"Not that I'm aware of, but maybe there should be. Doesn't Phoenix have an ordinance against smoking in restaurants?" he asked, waving his hand around to clear away a plume of smoke from the cigar of a customer standing behind us.

"If you say that any louder, you're going to start a riot. This is the last refuge in town for smokers," I answered.

"Why do you come here? You don't smoke, do you?"

"No, I don't, but I have a soft spot in my heart for society's outcasts, and smokers are the lepers of the twenty-first century,"

The hostess interrupted to tell us she had a table for us. Like the waitresses at DeRoy's, the hostess was wearing a stained nylon dress and a well-worn cardigan. The only difference was that her Rockports were black rather than white. Black Rockports were the formal attire at DeRoy's.

She seated us at a relatively quiet table in the back. After we placed our order (sirloin steak and fries for both of us), I got down to business. "What did you find out in the evidence room?"

Bryan sighed, and the strain I had seen earlier returned to his face.

"I found nothing," he said.

I was engulfed by a wave of disappointment. I was hoping the evidence room would provide some answers, one way or the other.

"You couldn't find *anything* to help us out?" I asked.

"That's not what I said. I said I didn't find anything. Nothing. Five boxes filled with baggies of cocaine were taken from Janner's car. The boxes and the drugs should have been in the safe. I found the boxes, but they're all empty."

CHAPTER FOURTEEN

I sat back and tried to absorb the implications of what Bryan had said. If the drugs were missing, someone from the sheriff's department or the county attorney's office most likely took them, and once the drug evidence was in the safe, only the sheriff, the county attorney, and Bryan had access to it.

"Did you find the chain-of-custody records?" I asked.

Bryan shook his head. "Even if it was there, I'm pretty sure whoever took the drugs didn't sign in and write "removal of drugs for personal gain" in the 'purpose' column."

"That's not what I meant," I said. "I was wondering whether the drugs were missing before they made it into the safe and that's why the charges were reduced."

"There's no way I wouldn't have heard about it if the evidence was lost or stolen before it even made it into the safe," said Bryan with conviction. "I was involved in the arrest, remember? Also, if the charges were reduced because the drugs disappeared after they were put in the safe, I would know about that too. Internal Affairs would have been all over me and everyone else in my office and yours, and security around the evidence room sure as heck would have been increased to more than what it is now."

"The only possibility left is that the drugs disappeared after they were put in the safe, but no one discovered that they were missing, until now, that is. How come no one noticed they were gone?" I ruminated for a while before answering my own question. "Let's assume Janner is charged with a felony. As in any criminal case, the evidence would be subject to review by defense counsel, and even an attorney from the overworked public defender's office would take a felony charge involving this amount of drugs seriously enough to make the effort to review the evidence.

"However, we are all assuming the initial charge was a felony that got reduced due to an evidentiary defect. What if Janner was charged with a misdemeanor from the outset? If that was the case, a public defender would not bother to look at the evidence unless and until the matter went to trial, and with drastically reduced charges like in the Janner case, no way would the defendant go to trial. He'd happily plead guilty to the reduced charges and go on his merry way. It could be months before anyone noticed the drugs were missing, if ever."

"Again, let me point out that the sheriff, the county attorney, and I are the only ones with direct access to the safe. Since, out of the three of us, I am the one with no power or influence, political or otherwise, guess who the fall guy will be once they find out the drugs are missing." He shook his head. "I'm screwed any way you look at it."

"Not necessarily," I said excitedly. "You said yourself that anyone can get into the safe provided they have written authorization from the county attorney or the sheriff. That means a lot more people than you think could have been in that safe.

"We need to find the chain-of-custody report for the Janner evidence, and, if the report shows the drugs made it into the safe—and based on what you said, it's almost certain they did—then we need to get the names of everyone who signed in at the guard's station after that. Do you know where the sign-in sheets are kept?"

"After each shift the guard on duty turns the sheets from his shift over to the filing clerk in the administrative office on the third floor, and they go into a locked file cabinet. After-hours the guards put the sheets in a box behind the counter, and they're filed first thing the next morning."

"Tomorrow can you get access to the sign-in sheets covering the period from the date Janner was arrested until now?" I asked.

Bryan smiled, and it struck me again how good looking he was. I felt an urge to run my fingers through his wavy blond hair.

"I think I can do that," he said, still smiling. "I took the filing clerk, Stacy, out a few times. I'm pretty sure she still has a thing for me. I'll get the file cabinet key from her."

The impulse to run my fingers through his hair turned into a desire to grab one of his lousy locks and jerk hard.

Fortunately the waitress interrupted us before I could act anything out. She slammed our plates down in front of us, upsetting my water glass and tipping over a sugar bowl in the process. I ordered a glass of wine before she could take off to wreak destruction on another table. Emboldened by my example, Bryan got in a request for ketchup, and she responded by grabbing a ketchup bottle out of the hand of a diner in the adjacent booth and handing it to Bryan. "Give it back to him when you're through," she ordered, indicating the man with a toss of her head. He waved weakly at us.

"Man," said Bryan. "These waitresses are tough. Maybe we should recruit for my department out of here."

Our waitress delivered my wine surprisingly fast. I had a suspicion she'd liberated it from another table.

Bryan ploughed through his steak. His mood had improved measurably, but I wasn't sure if this was because of the food or because we had at least part of a plan. Even if Bryan managed to get the sign-in lists, I still needed to find the chain-of-custody report. Despite Bryan's confidence that there was no way the drugs could have disappeared before they were put in the safe, and even though I had no reason to believe he wasn't telling the truth, I wasn't ready to trust him completely. Plus, my attorney-mindset compelled me to find corroborative evidence.

Bryan steered the conversation toward the normal kind of chitchat between two people just getting to know each other. He asked me about my job in Chicago and how I came to decide to move to Phoenix. He was flatteringly attentive to my answers and seemed especially interested in the experience I had at the Lazy ZZ, the Tucson dude ranch where I'd found Ralph. Admittedly, though, the dude ranch story is pretty good.

When it was my turn to do the questioning, I found out Bryan had been with the sheriff's department for ten years, was in the armed services before that, and hailed originally from upstate New York. He'd been married and divorced while in Phoenix but had no children. His ex-wife worked as a dispatcher in the sheriff's department.

With an ex-wife and ex-girlfriends floating around the office everywhere (I was pretty sure Stacy wasn't the only one), I wondered how he got any work done. I, on the other hand, made it a policy to never date co-workers because things inevitably got messy. Of course, during the years of my partnership with Randall in Chicago, this policy was never tested by even the slightest temptation. Randall and I were the only attorneys in the firm, and our support staff consisted of three secretaries and a paralegal, all of whom were women. The only chemistry between Randall and me was along the lines of chemical warfare.

I had hardly touched my food by the time Bryan polished off the last of his fries. My wine had disappeared quite quickly, however. When he asked about my lack of appetite, I told him I wasn't hungry after the huge hamburger I'd had at lunch. I flagged down our waitress and asked her to bring me a doggy bag. Ralph would be thrilled.

As we left the restaurant Bryan asked if I wanted to go somewhere else for a nightcap, but I was tired and I still had to talk to Cal, so I begged off.

"I'd better call it a night," I said. "It's been a long day, and I get the feeling tomorrow's going to be even longer."

"You're right. I should get home too," said Bryan, some of the gloominess returning to his voice.

I immediately felt sorry for being such a buzzkill.

When we got to my car I turned to face him, and said, "Don't worry, Bryan. We'll get this thing figured out, and everything will be fine."

As I reached for the door handle, he grabbed my hand, raised it to his lips, and kissed it. I felt a tingle in the pit of my stomach.

"Thank you," he said. He waited until I was safely inside my car before walking away.

I reminded myself of Stacy and the ex-wife in dispatch, and of my rule against office romances. *But technically he's not with your office,* a little voice in my head rationalized. *He's with the sheriff's department.* I told the little voice to shut up.

I called Cal to let him know I was coming. He sounded relieved to hear my voice.

When I got to my condo complex, I parked on the street, remembering my creepy experience with Alan in the garage that morning, and then took the elevator to the second floor. Even if Cal hadn't told me which unit was his, I could have figured it out. I could hear Ralph barking as soon as I got off the elevator. The door of unit 206 had barely opened in response to my knock when Ralph came rushing out and hurled himself at my legs. It's nice to have someone care that much about you, even if in this case that "someone" was a large, furry dog with a cold, wet nose and bad breath.

Cal ushered Ralph and me into his condo. I wasn't surprised to see Macy sitting on the couch in the living room. I sat next to her, and Ralph plopped down with his head on my feet, gazing at me worshipfully.

"The doggy sure missed you," said Macy. "He's been standing at that door all night. He went nuts when he heard the elevator door open. He knew it was you right away."

I patted Ralph on the head. "He's very loyal." I looked down at my shredded nylons, and reasoned that having to buy hosiery by the carton was a small price to pay for such loyalty.

Cal handed me a glass of white wine and sat across from me in a comfortable-looking club chair. His expression was solemn.

"Kate, I have reason to believe that Rantwist's crusading conservatism may just be a cover for something more serious," he said.

I had to suppress a smile. Cal sounded just like Jack Webb in *Dragnet*.

"Oh?" I said.

"I can't tell you why I think so, yet," he said, still in his Jack Webb persona. "I'm waiting to hear back from some friends of mine at the FBI. I asked them to track down some information for me. In the meantime, you need to stay away from your office. Things could get ugly. Call in sick tomorrow or something."

"I appreciate your concern, Cal, but the article in the newspaper today pretty much blew the cover off of Rantwist's penchant for overcharging certain defendants, and there's no reason to believe anyone at the office knows about my interest in the Janner case. Besides, the fact is that aside from a couple of cases of overcharging and undercharging, I know nothing about Rantwist's activities. I'm not a threat to anyone."

Cal looked frustrated. He probably wasn't expecting any resistance to his advice. "Just do what I say," he said. "Stay at home tomorrow, and don't talk to anybody."

I turned to Macy for help, but she just nodded grimly in agreement with Cal.

I secretly thought he was acting a bit full of himself and was probably overreacting to a minor issue so he could take center stage for a while. I noticed it was working on Macy, at least. She was staring at him with unabashed adoration.

"Thanks for the advice, Cal. I will consider it seriously. But right now, Ralph and I need to get home and go to bed. Be sure to let me know what your FBI friends come up with," I said. I couldn't see how I was going to change his mind, so I figured an excuse and a hasty exit was my best strategy. In truth, though, I was genuinely tired, and Ralph looked like he was barely holding on. His eyes were drooping, and he'd shown no interest in the doggy bag sitting in my lap. The last part worried me. Maybe I should have him checked out by the vet.

"Well, you don't have to worry about feeding Ralphy," said Macy. "The doggy ate everything in the refrigerator. I never even knew doggies could eat lettuce."

At least one mystery was solved, and I didn't need to take Ralph to the vet.

CHAPTER FIFTEEN

Back at my condo I changed out of my work clothes into a pair of cutoffs and a T-shirt with "Little Miss Sunshine" printed on it. The staff at my Chicago firm had given it to me last year as a joke.

Ralph was standing by the front door when I came out of the bedroom. "You have to go to the bathroom again, don't you?" I said accusingly. "If I've told you once, I've told you a million times—lettuce is roughage. It goes through you like a shot, and it takes everything else along with it."

I wasn't sure if I'd told Ralph this a million times before, or even once before for that matter. In any event, based on the look of quiet desperation in his eyes, remonstrations at this point would not be effective.

I shoved a pair of flip-flops on my feet and grabbed Ralph's leash. Punishing him for overindulgence by not letting him go out was bound to end badly, and I didn't want to have to scrape dog duty off the floor tiles the next morning.

It was a bit after ten by this time. The street was relatively quiet, and the temperature was surprisingly pleasant. We turned off the main drag into a residential area nearby, and the noise level dropped even further. Ralph wasted little time in finding a lawn to decorate, but it was so pleasant out, I decided to walk him around the neighborhood some more. Besides, I needed time to think.

Bryan would take a look at the sign-in sheets tomorrow morning, but I would need to find the answer to the chain-of-custody issue. I dismissed the possibility of interviewing the other officers involved in the arrest and everyone else who'd handled the evidence before it was deposited in the safe. That would take too much time and raise too much suspicion.

I wondered if there was any other place we could find a copy of the chain-of-custody report. Something in the back of my mind gnawed at me. *A while ago MJ had mentioned something about office paperwork processing. What was it?*

Then I remembered. She'd said that everything coming into the office was scanned into the computer. Even if the chain-of-custody report was removed from the evidence box and the hard copy of the file, there still might be a copy in the computer file. The same thought was likely to occur to Rantwist, though. I needed to see the computer file for the Janner case ASAP, before the report was purged from the computer files, if it was not already gone.

I ran back to my condo, dragging Ralph behind me. (Ralph did not like to be hurried. He was not one of those dogs you see jogging with their owners in the morning. He was more of the "I'll watch while you exercise" variety of pet). I called MJ's cell phone as soon as we got back inside. A sleepy-sounding MJ answered after the eleventh ring.

"Who the hell is this?" she asked.

"It's Kate. Nice phone manners, by the way. Remind me to ask you to record the greeting on my voice mail."

"You woke me up," accused MJ, now sounding fully awake.

"Can you meet me at the office in an half hour?" I asked.

At first there was silence at her end.

"You're fucking kidding me," she finally said. "I barely make it to the office during regular hours."

"You'll get overtime for it," I said hopefully, trying to appeal to her base interests.

I heard a male voice in the background, presumably Mitchie's, followed by a resounding thwack and a yelp from Mitchie. A heated discussion followed.

MJ finally came back on the line. "Fine," she growled. "But I want double overtime pay. Plus, I'm thinking of getting my navel pierced, and I want you to pay for it."

"Agreed." I brought MJ up to speed on what had happened and what I was thinking, and ended with an emphatic "Now get moving."

I hung up, grabbed my purse, and ran to the door, where I slid to a stop. Ralph had planted himself in the middle of the doorway. Apparently he figured he'd lost me once today, and not even another refrigerator load of food could make him go through that again.

Exasperated, I grabbed his leash and clipped it to his collar, and we set off together.

Traffic was light, which was a good thing, because Ralph was making it difficult to drive; he kept trying to crawl over to the driver's side and sit on my lap. He was having serious attachment issues.

I parked in front of my building, hauled an unenthusiastic Ralph out of the car, and tied him up at the bottom of the railing on the front steps. After digging around, I found the keys at the bottom of my purse. They had been issued to me my first day of work, but I hadn't used them before so it took me a while to figure out which one was for the front door. After some fumbling accompanied by whispered profanities, I unlocked the door. It killed me to leave Ralph outside in light of his delicate mental condition, but it was bad enough I was sneaking in after hours. Sneaking in with a hundred-fifty-pound dog was just that much worse. "You'll be okay, boy," I reassured him in a soft voice. "I'll be back in a jiffy." Ralph wagged his tail a couple of times, but he did not look convinced.

The building, like all empty buildings at night, was eerily quiet, and each footstep echoed loudly for what seemed like an unnecessarily long time.

I expected to see a guard in the lobby, but the guard's station was empty. Sloppy security was really working in my favor today.

I took the steps instead of the elevator, figuring that punching a button and waiting for an elevator was inconsistent with the underlying theory of covert operations. I was out of breath by the time I reached my office, and had concluded that I needed to work an exercise plan into my schedule. I unlocked my office door and flopped into my chair like a rag doll—if rag dolls panted like overweight retrievers, that is.

I had not turned on the lights, but the streetlamps outside provided a little illumination. At least enough for me to identify the outline of a figure standing in the hallway outside.

"MJ?" I whispered.

The shadow slid sideways through the doorway.

"Hello, Kate," said Alan, as though it were just another day at work.

"Did you follow me here?" I demanded. I no longer bothered to whisper since the person I was trying to avoid was standing in front of me.

"I did. It was quite entertaining. At first I thought your dog was driving. Then I realized you were next to him. You two are very, very close. I'm guessing some heavy petting was going on."

The play on words would have been cute coming from someone else, but coming from Alan, it sounded sick.

"Get out, Alan, before I call the police and have you hauled out of here."

He laughed, which wasn't a good omen. Alan's sense of humor was somewhere between twisted and psychotic.

"Are you meeting someone here?" he asked calmly. Obviously he was not impressed by my threat to call the police.

"No," I lied. "I couldn't sleep, so I decided to get some work done."

"Why did you call me MJ when you first saw me, then?" he persisted.

"Because you have the same profile," I shot back. *Good save*, I chided myself. *You just told a short, sunken-chested twerp you had mistaken him for a full-bosomed amazon.*

I couldn't see Alan's face very well, but I knew he was smirking.

"In any event," he said, "I'm glad you're here. I want to show you something. Come with me."

"No," I said.

"Yes," he countered. He waved something in his hand at me. It gleamed in the dim light. It was a gun.

The man is insane, I thought wildly. Then I corrected myself. *He's more insane than I thought.* I fought back an urge to laugh hysterically. We already had one nut too many in the room.

Alan grabbed my arm and pulled me out of my chair.

"Where are we going?" I asked shakily.

"Someplace you've been before," he said, shoving me down the hallway in front of him.

I did not find the promise of familiar surroundings reassuring.

We followed the same route I had taken earlier in the day when I'd gone searching for Bryan. Alan walked so close to me that I could feel his hot breath on my neck. His body odor, which, as usual, smelled like old sweat and spoiled food, was almost refreshing compared to his intermittent blasts of halitosis. Every so often he would push me impatiently so I would walk faster. After each shove I would speed up at first, and then gradually slow down again. I did not feel the same sense of urgency as he.

As had been the case in the building lobby, there was no guard on duty in the basement hallway. We went through the gate without impediment. Since Alan was not operating under the same covert operation guidelines I had been, we took the elevator rather than the stairs, and got out on the fifth floor.

At this point I was pretty sure where we were headed.

He marched me down the hall, unlocked the door of the unguarded evidence room, and turned on the lights. He shoved me inside ahead of him and shut the door behind us. Keeping his gun trained on me, he walked over to a safe the size of a bank vault and, with the ease of familiarity, punched a series of numbers into a keypad on the door.. Neither Bryan nor I had been aware that Alan had access to the evidence room and safe, but I wasn't surprised. Rantwist probably gave him the key and the safe code.

Alan opened the safe door and motioned with his gun for me to go in. He followed me and pointed to a large file cabinet in the corner of the room.

There was a space about a foot wide between the cabinet and the wall.

"The thing I want to show you is behind the cabinet," he said, in the same tone a person might use to point out new drapes in the kitchen.

Glancing nervously at Alan and his gun, I moved to where I could see behind the cabinet, having no idea what to expect. The first thing I saw was a pair of legs. My eyes followed the legs up to a head. I gasped and stepped back. Bryan's body had been shoved behind the cabinet and lay in a position impossibly uncomfortable for a live person to endure.

I started to shake uncontrollably.

Alan, on the other hand, really seemed to be enjoying himself. His smirk had widened into a grin, and he was rocking on his feet like a kid who'd just won the spelling bee.

"Don't worry, lovely lady," he said. "He's not dead. Not yet, anyway. I found him in the third-floor administrative offices earlier this evening. He gave me some trouble, so I had to give him something to calm him down. We need to wait for the drugs to clear out of his system before I kill you both, so no questions will be raised by the autopsy."

"Why are you doing this?" I blurted.

Alan actually looked pleased that I had asked. "I'd be happy to explain everything to you. That will give us something to talk about while we wait for sleeping beauty here to wake up."

Alan took a quick look at Bryan to make sure he was still unconscious, then pulled me out of the vault and slammed the heavy door. "Let's go back to the hall for a minute."

Like I had a choice. I preceded him into the hallway, where he directed me to the back of the guard station. A blank video monitor stood on a table behind a half wall.

"Take a seat. We're going to watch a little television," he said.

When I hesitated, he grabbed me by the shoulder and pushed me down into a chair in front of the monitor. Looking distastefully at his hand on my shoulder, I noticed for the first time that Alan was wearing thin latex gloves. I had mixed feelings about this. On the one hand, the gloves prevented his fingerprints from showing up anywhere, thereby making it difficult to prove he was ever in the evidence room or vault. On the other hand, the gloves meant Alan's cooty-covered hands couldn't actually come in contact with me.

"Plug it in," he demanded, pointing to an electrical cord in back of the monitor. I did as he said.

"Usually the monitor records all movement on the Floor," Alan explained in a sing-song story telling voice, "but tonight some very evil people broke into the building and unplugged the system so they could rob evidence from the safe without being detected."

Great, I thought. *And of course now my fingerprints are on the electrical cord.*

"I want you to watch the monitor and what I will refer to as Exhibit A," he continued.

A stack of video tapes lay to the left of the monitor. A time and date were written in black magic marker on the spine of each of them. Alan pulled out the one with today's date and shoved it into a tape deck under the counter. He hit the play button with a flourish.

A split screen showed the inside of the evidence room and the inside of the safe. I watched as Bryan entered the evidence room and opened the safe. The inside image of the safe was a bit grainy and dark, but I could see Bryan scanning the case names written on the boxes, then pulling out a box containing what I figured was probably the Janner evidence. Again, the dark image made it difficult to see detail, but I could make out Bryan searching through the evidence, then replacing the box and leaving. His body blocked some of what he'd been doing with his hands.

Alan popped the tape out, selected another tape from the stack, and put it into the tape deck.

"Exhibit B," he said.

This tape showed the hallway. I watched myself get off the elevator, walk toward the evidence room, then flatten against the wall when I spotted the guard. Next it showed me disappearing into the men's room with Bryan following me in a few seconds later.

"The guard, Deputy Sheriff Banff, who, coincidentally, is a friend of mine"—*Alan has a friend? Who could have seen that coming?*—"got suspicious. He called me and told me he saw you two reconnoitering. I came up, took a look at the safe, and found the drugs in the Janner evidence box missing. You can't imagine how shocked I was."

Something in his voice made me turn to look at him. His eyes sparkled with enjoyment, making him look even more deranged than usual.

"You and Rantwist took the drugs, didn't you?" I said.

Alan slapped me. Hard. Apparently I had hit a hot button.

"How dare you impugn my reputation. County attorneys are temporary employees only interested in using their position as a stepping-stone to higher office," he said, his voice shaking. "They don't have the focus and commitment required to pull off anything like this. They are of no help to me. Even were that not the case, I would never stoop to joining forces with someone like Rantwist. He's an idiot. He's convinced Phoenix is the modern Sodom and Gomorrah and that God is his personal advisor. He's out to purge the city of prostitutes, queers, and wiener wavers. Since there's nothing in the Bible about drug dealers, he couldn't care less about them."

"Wiener wavers?" I couldn't help it. I had to ask.

"The naked guy on Third and Central."

"Ah. Right."

"I've been the real power in the county attorney's office for over twelve years, and no one, but no one, gets in my way," Alan continued. "I do have *assistants* outside the county attorney's office that help me out my projects, but they work for me, not the other way around. I am grateful to Rantwist in one respect, though. His idiotic crusade has diverted attention away from drug crimes, so it's been easier than usual to remove drugs from the safe."

"So who gave you access to the evidence room and the safe if Rantwist isn't in on this?"

A voice from behind us said, "I did."

I had never met the man standing in the hallway behind Alan, but I had no trouble recognizing him. Sheriff Hal Harmon loved publicity, and his face appeared regularly in the media.

"Alan, what the hell is taking so long?" the sheriff asked. Although Alan had no doubt meant to include the sheriff as one of the "assistants" to whom he had referred, it was pretty clear that Harmon was the alpha dog here.

Alan shrugged apologetically. "I had to drug Turner. We need to wait for the drugs to work out of his system so they don't show up in an autopsy."

"Where is he now?" asked the sheriff.

"In the evidence room. I should probably go check on him. He may be coming around by now. Could you watch her, sir?" said Alan, jerking his head toward me.

"With pleasure." Harmon reached under his jacket and produced a long barreled, pearl handled revolver that looked liked something Annie Oakley would have used in Buffalo Bill's Wild West Show.

Alan trotted off to the evidence room, and the sheriff got comfortable, raising a hip and resting one of his his buttocks on the guard's desk.

"So you're the new prosecutor. I heard you were good looking, but the descriptions don't give you justice."

The timing of his compliment was off. His delivery would be much better if he wasn't pointing a gun at me.

"I thought you hated drug dealers," I said. I figured at this point I was dead meat anyway, so why not die well informed.

"Let's just say I want as many of them arrested as possible," said the sheriff, smiling. "We need to constantly restock our inventory. Sales have really been good."

Alan still hadn't returned, even though it should have taken him mere seconds to check on Bryan.

The sheriff stood up impatiently and moved closer to the evidence room door. "Alan, what the hell is going on? Let's wrap this up. I need to catch a few hours of shut-eye. I've got to give a speech at the Citizens Against Crime breakfast at eight a.m."

"Bring her in, then. I'll handle it now," Alan called out, his voice somewhat muffled by the thick door.

The sheriff motioned for me to get up. "Come on, sweetie. It's showtime."

I took my time standing, hoping without rational basis for rescue.

"Hurry up," the sheriff growled. "I don't want to arrive at that breakfast with bags under my eyes."

I walked ahead of him into the evidence room and immediately looked around for Bryan. I did not see him, but I did see Alan, who was lying in the middle of the room. His arms and legs were tied together like a roped calf and his mouth was taped shut.

Things happened quickly after that. First Bryan appeared from behind the file cabinet. Next, MJ, with Sam hard on her heels, rushed into the evidence room. The sheriff fired a shot, and MJ went down, clutching her leg. Bryan wrestled the sheriff for the gun while Sam attacked the sheriff from behind. I ran to MJ and tried to pull her out of the room to safety. The sheriff managed to break away from Bryan and Sam and took off down the hall. Bryan started to go after him, but Sam yelled for him to stop. "I'll let the agents downstairs know he's coming," said Sam. "Let them handle this."

"Agents?" asked Bryan.

Sam pulled a small walkie-talkie out of his waistband and spoke to someone at the other end.

"No one will dare stop him," I cried hysterically. "He's the sheriff, for God's sake."

Sam smiled thinly. "And the boys downstairs are from the FBI. Believe me; they won't be impressed with the sheriff's position."

"FBI agents?" said Bryan, sounding thoroughly bewildered.

Sam looked toward the growing pool of blood around MJ. "MJ!" he called out in distress as he moved quickly to her side. All of us huddled around her. Sam removed his expensive Armani jacket and handed it to me without hesitation. I tied its sleeves around the top of her thigh in a rough tourniquet. Trying to keep the hysteria out of my voice I asked her again and again if she was okay until, after about my twentieth iteration, she said, "Shut up." Her voice was weak and barely audible, but her eyes were open, and she was looking at me with consternation. "How can I answer you if you don't wait long enough to let me get a word in edgewise?"

Four men wearing blue and gold FBI jackets crowded into the room. Two of them got on either side of Alan's supine form and one cut through the metal strips binding his arms and legs together while the other ripped the tape off his mouth. Alan yelped, then pointed to me and Bryan and screamed "Arrest them! They are the evildoers, not me!" The agents appeared unmoved by Alan's pleas. They hauled him to his feet and cuffed him, then marched him out the door, reciting his Miranda rights along the way.

In the meantime, the other agents had shooed us away from MJ and knelt beside her. One produced a medical kit and proceeded to replace my makeshift tourniquet with the real thing. He then pulled out a syringe filled with clear fluid.

"What's that?" MJ asked anxiously.

"Painkiller," said the man with the syringe.

"Cool," said MJ.

The stretcher arrived with the next wave of FBI agents, and we watched as they carried MJ into the elevator.

"Whoopee!" she chortled as the elevator doors closed.

"That painkiller must be primo stuff," said Sam enviously.

Bryan caught one of the remaining FBI agents by the arm. "Did your guys get Harmon?" he asked.

The agent snorted. "Yeah. With no shots fired. He ran through the basement to the next building and escaped through the front door, but he slipped on a big pile of dogshit when he was running down the front steps. We found him on the ground, covered with poop, and swearing non-stop. The biggest dog I've ever seen was sitting next to him trying to lick his face."

Ralph, I thought.

"It's a good thing, too," continued the agent, "because we didn't have that exit covered. We didn't know about the basement corridor between the two buildings."

"How? Why were you ...?" I started to ask, but Bryan interrupted me.

"Let's you, me, and Sam go somewhere we can all talk. Between the three of us we should be able to figure out everything that's happened tonight," he said. "How about we go to your place, Kate?"

I nodded.

"Sam, does that work for you?" he asked.

"Sure. But I need to make a phone call before we get there. There's someone else that should be part of our discussion group."

Bryan turned to the FBI agent and asked, "Is it okay with you guys if we leave? I can give you the address of the place we're going"

"Don't worry about it," said the agent. "We can take your statements tomorrow." He looked at his watch and corrected himself. "I mean later today."

I looked at the wall clock. It was just after midnight.

Bryan walked me to my car, stopping at the building entrance on the way long enough for me to collect Ralph, who, needless to say, was overjoyed to see me. He looked pretty natty. Someone had tied a scarf around his neck with "FBI Agent" printed on it. I noticed his breath smelled suspiciously like a Slim Jim.

"Are you okay to drive?" asked Bryan.

I nodded. I still felt somewhat numb, and the parts of me that weren't numb were exhausted. However, the streets were so empty at this hour, even if I chose to take a little nap behind the wheel, there was little danger I would hit anyone.

Miraculously I managed to keep my eyes open for the entire trip, thanks in large part to Ralph's constant face licking, and we arrived safely at my condo complex. When we got to my front door, I heard voices inside and stopped to listen just to be on the safe side. Once I identified one of the voices as belonging to Bryan, I figured it was okay to go in. Besides, what could happen? I had Ralph the Wonder Dog with me.

I walked in with Ralph at my heels but got no further than the foyer. I sucked my breath in sharply as the all too familiar feelings of shock and surprise swept over me. Macy and Sam were sitting on the couch. Bryan was sitting, somewhat lopsidedly, on the dog bed-*cum*-futon. The cause of my startled reaction was sitting between Macy and Sam. She was larger than Sam and a lot larger than Macy. She was impeccably dressed in a Chanel suit. Her blond hair hung in soft curls down to her shoulders. She was wearing a bit too much makeup for my taste, but even in my shocked condition, I coveted her six-inch designer heels.

The woman stood and extended her hand. I crossed the room and we shook hands which required no effort on my part since my whole body had the shaking thing down as a result of the events of the last twenty-four hours.

"I believe we've met before," she said in a deep, sultry voice.

We had, and I had recognized her as soon as I saw her on the couch. She was the woman suspected of the burglary of Albert Kenly's office, the one who'd tripped over Ralph.

She reached up and removed her long blond hair.

I looked at her, now him, closely.

"Cal?" I ventured.

"Righto," he said in his regular Cal voice. "You'd better take a seat. There's a lot you need to hear."

Since all the seats in the living room were taken, I dragged a chair out of the kitchen and sat down. Ralph immediately flopped down and rested his head on my feet, a position that had become his default setting.

"Go ahead," I said to Cal, swooshing my arm in invitation.

"Although it doesn't have a lot to do with what happened tonight, I think I'd better explain why I am dressed the way I am first."

I nodded my head in agreement. I, too, thought this was a wise starting point, because I was having a hard time focusing on what Cal was saying. My eyes kept drifting from his face to his clothes and then to those magnificent shoes and back again.

"I used to work undercover in the FBI," Cal continued. "Disguising as a woman was my specialty. Not only was I good at it, but also I found I was more comfortable working in women's clothes. Plus, women's fashion gives one so many more style options."

Macy, Sam, and I all nodded in agreement with the last statement.

"I continued wearing women's clothes after retiring from the FBI, but only at night, and never around my daughter or her kids. She's got enough to deal with," Cal said, smiling ruefully.

"Are you the Paris Hilton Bandit?" I asked.

"Yes, but I did *not* rob that convenience store. I went in to get a soda. When the clerk opened the cash register to get my change, she said she broke her nail on the register and asked if I had a nail file. I dug one out of my purse and tried to hand it to her, but she put on a big show of being scared, and handed me my change. Then I saw her put all the rest of the cash in the register in her pocket. I didn't rob the store. She did. Then that lousy little bitch had the audacity …"

"What about the burglary of Kenly's office?" I interrupted. Cal's righteous indignation over the convenience store episode was threatening to derail his train of thought. I wanted to keep him on track.

"That was the night you told Macy and me about the shenanigans going on at your office. Remember? We were here in your condo, enjoying a few drinks."

I disagreed with his reference to a "few" drinks. It was a minor discrepancy though, so I didn't bother to correct him.

"Later that night I got to thinking about things, and in my business, rather, in my *old* business, if we wanted to find the bad guy, we usually started by following the money trail. Kenly contributed a lot of money to both the sheriff's and Rantwist's political campaigns, but that made no sense to me. Kenly is a real estate developer. Real estate guys are always looking to get friends in public office who will take their side on construction industry–related issues, like rezoning, construction permits, and building codes. The sheriff's department and the county attorney's office have nothing to do with that kind of stuff. It would make more sense for a developer to back a city councilman or state legislator. These are the folks who make decisions impacting Kenly's industry. So why throw money away to help elect a sheriff and a county attorney? What's the payback?

"I knew Kenly's office was just up the street. Since it was so convenient location-wise, I figured I'd take a stroll over and see what I could find that might throw some light on the issue. I changed into my 'business' clothes and walked to his building. Breaking and entering was a piece of cake. The guard was too busy watching a baseball game on his monitor to notice me. I snuck up the stairs to Kenly's office and picked the door lock."

"With your ever-handy nail file?" I interjected.

"As a matter of fact, yes," Cal said, looking slightly annoyed by the interruption. He went back to the story where he'd left off. "I took my time going through Kenly's files once I was inside the office. While I was sneaking through the lobby, I heard the television announcer say the game was only in the fifth inning, so I figured there was no hurry. I found a ledger book at the bottom of a locked filing cabinet, underneath a pile of Kenly's personal files—you know, tax returns, mortgage information, that kind of stuff. That's when that idiot guard walked in. I grabbed the ledger, shoved it into the waistband of my panty hose, decked the guard, and took off. I got out of the building without a problem, but I tripped over Ralph when I was running down the sidewalk, as you may recall.

"Macy was awake when I got back to my condo. She tried to clock me with a vase. I think she thought I was a burglar."

Cal must have noticed the blank look on some of the faces in the room.

"I forgot to mention," he said. "Macy came to my condo after we left Kate's. We ... ah ... talked for a while, and then she fell asleep on the couch."

More like she passed out on the couch, I thought.

Cal looked at Macy fondly and reached over to squeeze her hand.

"Cal's a great talker," simpered Macy.

"Anyway, after I got things straightened out with Macy, we took a look at the ledger I'd taken from Kenly's office. It showed that huge amounts of money were being deposited into the account of Kenly's development firm, a substantial percentage of which was then paid to people referred to only as a 'County Attorney Employee' and a 'Sheriff's Department Employee.' Based on Kate's descriptions of Rantwist and Alan, I thought there was a good chance one of them was the 'County Attorney Employee.' I had no idea who the 'Sheriff's Department Employee' was, however.

"I called up a friend at the FBI and passed the information on to him. He and his group thought the information provided by the ledger raised enough questions to warrant further investigation into the situation. His computer boys hacked into the electronic files of the county attorney's office and the sheriff's department and found a pattern of inconsistencies between the amount of drugs seized in a case, as reflected by the chain-of-custody report, and the level of charges brought by the county attorney's office against the dealer. In each case, the charges were greatly reduced due to 'deficiencies in evidentiary chain of custody.' Someone had deleted the chain-of-custody reports from the system, but the feds were able to recover some of them. None of the reports they found supported the reason given for the reduced charges. It had to be an inside job, though. No one on the outside would have either access to the evidence and reports or the ability to manipulate the charges.

Apparently insider thefts of drugs from law enforcement evidence rooms are pretty common, but the sheriff's operation was institutionalized and pretty sophisticated. "It looked like the thefts had occurred over a period of ten years or more. Since Rantwist was the new kid on the block, while it was possible he was involved in current thefts from the evidence room, it made more sense that people who had been on staff for a while had carried out the drug thefts." Cal looked pointedly at Bryan. "Alan, the sheriff, and a few others were likely candidates due to the length of time they'd held their jobs.

"In the meantime, Kate, you and Bryan were doing some snooping of your own, and , Bryan decided to check the time sheets for the guard station last night after you two had dinner."

"I wanted to find the time sheets right away instead of waiting until the next day," Bryan explained. "I figured the office would be empty until the guards came in to drop off their time sheets after the night shift, and after thinking about it, I really didn't want to have to deal with the file clerk in the morning. You see, Stacy and I used to date, and it's awkward for me to—"

"I believe I am speaking for all of when I say that none of us wants to hear about your past love life with Stacy," said Sam. That went double for me. "Skip the parts about what I'm sure was a multilayered relationship of great complexity with a woman who thinks alphabetical order is, as she put it to me one day, 'a fluid and living concept.'"

Bryan looked annoyed but continued with no further references to Stacy. "Anyway, I was looking through the files, and I didn't hear Alan come up behind me. I didn't even hear the door open. I don't know how the guy does it. I felt a sharp stabbing pain in my ass—sorry, buttock. It shocked the hell out of me. I turned around and saw Alan standing there with a syringe, and I threw a punch at him. That's the last thing I remember."

Cal was nodding as if Bryan had provided an important piece of the puzzle. "That fits in with what the FBI told me. They found a syringe on the floor of the administration office with traces of Rohypnol in it."

Sam looked over at Bryan. "You were hit with a dose of roofies? The date rape drug? I bet Alan had something in mind other than murder. I knew it! He probably had a crush on you, too," he said feelingly.

Bryan looked completely confused. "What? What are you talking about? And what do you mean Alan had a crush on me *too*?"

Cal shook his head and cleared his throat, "Allow me to continue with the story," he said.

We all dutifully returned our attention to Cal, although Bryan still looked disturbed.

"It seems Alan managed to get Bryan into the elevator, take him to the fifth floor, and drag him into the evidence room. We think, but don't know, that somehow Alan got wind of either the FBI investigation or Kate and Bryan's unofficial investigation, or both, and, when he saw Bryan searching for time sheets, came up with a plan to blame the evidence thefts on Bryan."

"So why drag Katie into all of this? She's such a nice girl. It don't make sense," commented Macy.

"He'd seen Bryan and her near the evidence room on the video monitor. He also knew they'd been together at lunch and dinner. He figured whatever Bryan knew, she knew too. After he put Bryan in the evidence room, he drove to Kate's condo, probably intending to kidnap her using Rohypnol again. He must have been thrilled to death when Kate left in her car and drove to the very place he wanted her to be."

Macy leaned over and patted me on the knee. "Don't blame yourself, sweetie. You didn't know. Mr. Smarty-pants here shoulda been watchin' you, or shoulda had one of his FBI friends watch you."

"Smarty-*skirt*," corrected Sam.

"I don't remember you making that suggestion at the time," Cal shot back at Macy.

At this rate, between Cal's verbosity and all the interruptions from the audience, his explanation was going to take hours. It had already taken far too long.

"Cal, maybe leave out the detail and the surmise," I suggested. "I think we're all tired and getting snippy. Maybe just tell us how the FBI got there. We can pretty much fill in the blanks on the rest."

But Cal was enjoying the spotlight. He wasn't about to give it up that easily. He made us wait while he freshened up his lipstick before continuing.

"I was on my way to the garage to get some, um, potentially self-incriminating stuff out of my car when I saw an SUV with county plates pull out and follow Kate's car. I had a bad feeling about it and alerted the FBI. The FBI guys were already watching the county government buildings downtown while they waited for a search warrant. They spotted Kate parking her car near the county attorney's building and watched her enter the front door. Then Alan pulled up, parked behind Kate's car, and followed her in. The FBI agent I spoke to was more descriptive. He said he saw Alan 'slink along after Kate like the Boris Badinoff guy in *Rocky and Bullwinkle*.' The agents figured something was going down, so they called in for backup. Things got a little complicated when MJ drove up and went into the building. By the time she got to Kate's office, though, Alan had already escorted Kate to the evidence room."

"When MJ couldn't find you, and you didn't answer your cell phone, she got nervous and called me," said Sam. "When I showed up, I guess the FBI thought things were getting a little out of hand. They stopped me before I got to Kate's office, and I told them why I was there. Then they found MJ, and she filled them in on what Kate had told her on the phone about the missing evidence, Bryan's plan to take a look at the sign-in sheets for the evidence room, and Kate's idea to check the computer files. Since Kate was not in her office or at MJ's computer terminal, they figured all the action was taking place in the sheriff's department, so we all headed over there."

Bryan picked up the story again. "While all this was going on, I was zonked out, crammed in back of a file cabinet. I had started to come to a little bit when Alan and Kate first came in the evidence room, but I was still too out of it to do anything constructive. Later I heard the sheriff's voice in the hallway, and while I couldn't make out what he was saying, the fact that he was there at all was suspicious.

When Alan came back into the vault I was ready for him. I had a couple of those metal strips we use to hold the evidence boxes together and a roll of masking tape. I jumped Alan as soon as the door opened and he went down in a dead faint. I had just finished trussing him up when the sheriff called out to him. I answered, trying as best I could to sound like Alan so he wouldn't get suspicious."

Bryan made it sound as if imitating Alan's voice was a huge stretch.

"I think you sounded just like Alan. But then, you two are similar in so many ways." I couldn't help it. The opportunity to tease him was irresistible.

He responded by sticking his tongue out at me. We were two of a kind when it came to mature expressions of emotion.

Sam looked back and forth at the two of us. "Now, children," he said. "Be nice to each other."

I was mildly annoyed at being reprimanded by someone who'd incautiously implied that Alan had the hots for Bryan.

Bryan said nothing, so Sam, taking this as a sign that Bryan was finished with his part of the story, continued.

"MJ and I were coming up the elevator probably about the time Bryan was doing his Alan impression. We were supposed to stick with the FBI agents, but they were busy searching the administrative offices on the third floor and weren't paying attention to us. At that point they were pretty convinced that Kate, Bryan, and Alan were no longer in the building. The agents didn't know for sure yet if Bryan and Kate were in cahoots with Alan or were Alan's victims, but they hadn't found a sign of any of them, and if they *were* in cahoots, staying in the building after the FBI arrived would be too risky. MJ and I felt the agents were on the wrong track, and it was possible you guys were being held somewhere in the building against your wills. We knew about the missing evidence, so we decided to sneak away and go up to the fifth floor to see if anything was happening there. When we got out of the elevator, we heard voices coming from down by the evidence room. I wanted to call the FBI guys—they'd given me one of their walkie-talkies—but MJ barged ahead of me down the hall. I ran after her, and we came around the corner and saw the sheriff going into the evidence room with a gun in Kate's back. MJ ran and hurled herself at him. That's when he shot her. I came in right behind MJ, and you know what happened after that."

We all fell silent at the mention of the risk MJ took and her resulting injury. She may have acted precipitously, but in doing so she saved my and Bryan's lives.

Bryan was the first to break the silence, and thankfully changed the subject. "What about Kenly? Has he been picked up yet?"

"Apparently Alan is blabbing nonstop. Of course he's emphasizing the others' roles and his relative innocence. His defense is along the lines of 'they made me do it.' In any event, he's naming names, so there will likely be more arrests coming down the pike."

"That doesn't surprise me at all," said Bryan sleepily. He looked like he was about to doze off. Admittedly, the dog bed was incredibly comfortable. I'd never understood why Ralph didn't take to it.

"I guess I'd better be leaving," said Sam, who looked equally tired. Addressing me, he said, "I may be a little late to work tomorrow, or rather, today."

"I won't be there to notice," I said.

Cal and Macy stood to leave as well. I told Bryan he could sleep on the couch if he wanted, and he accepted the offer. Macy gave me a thumbs-up as she and Cal walked to the door.

I scrounged up some extra sheets, a pillow, and a blanket, and did a reasonable job of making up the couch. Bryan thanked me and moved wearily and with effort from the doggy bed to the couch. I could tell right away it wasn't going to work. The couch is one of those modern types where the legs and armrests are made of metal tubing. Bryan was too tall for the couch, so both his head and his legs smashed up against the uncomfortable metal.

"You look like a prisoner in Abu Ghraib," I said.

"Don't worry. I'm fine. It looks worse than it is," he said. Nanoseconds later he shouted "Goddammit, that hurt," when his head struck the metal as he tried to find a more comfortable position.

"Come on," I said. "Don't be a martyr. This is obviously not going to work." After a short pause, I added, "Why don't you sleep with me?"

Bryan sat up energetically. "Really?"

"I'm using the word 'sleep' in a literal sense. I have a king-size bed. You can retreat to your side, and I can retreat to mine, and 'ne'er in the 'tween to meet.'"

Of course, the "ne'er in the 'tween to meet" business went right out the window. Even with both of us exhausted, we were pretty damn good together. Ralph lay at the foot of the bed looking bored, which was kind of distracting, so we made him lie on the floor. Later on we let him back up and, after looking at me as if to say "What the hell was that about?", he curled up between us and fell asleep.

CHAPTER SIXTEEN

My internal alarm clock, still set on got-to-get-to-work time, woke me up at 7 a.m. Bryan was asleep, snoring softly. Ralph was also asleep, snoring loudly. Bryan's arms were wrapped around Ralph's neck, and they were lying together in the spoon position. I thought they looked kind of cute; weird, but cute.

I tiptoed to the bathroom, performed my morning ablutions, then went into the kitchen and made some coffee. I should have been exhausted, but I wasn't. I think I was still wired from all the activity last night.

Since Friday still qualified as a workday, I figured I might as well go into the office and accomplish something. With the mystery solved, and Alan gone, I should actually be able to focus on the job for which I was hired. I still had Rantwist's crusade to deal with, but that seemed small in comparison to what was sure to be a huge scandal involving the sheriff, Alan, and one of Phoenix's civic leaders.

I dressed quietly, although it occurred to me that my efforts to avoid disturbing the two sleeping princes were probably unnecessary. If Ralph's snoring didn't wake Bryan, nothing would.

I didn't have time to look at the newspaper, but I left it on the kitchen table for Bryan along with an empty cup and a note telling him where I was, inviting him to have some coffee, and asking that he walk Ralph.

I called the hospital en route to my office to check on MJ. The nurse said that the bullet had been removed from her leg and she was doing fine. She'd been asleep since her operation.

Things were relatively normal at the office, all things considered. Everyone had lots of questions, of course, especially about MJ, and I did the best I could to answer them. I was pleased to see that the staff had already started up a collection to send flowers to her at the hospital.

No one seemed to miss Alan.

I finally broke away and went into my office, closing the door behind me. Sam had loaned me his doorstop, and I shoved it into place. I wasn't feeling particularly antisocial, and Alan, MJ, and Sam were not around today to invade my privacy, but I wasn't taking any chances. If I didn't get some real work done, Rantwist would not need to look farther than my performance (or lack thereof) for an excuse to fire me.

I was absorbed in a second-degree murder file when I heard someone clear his throat. I looked up, startled. For the first time I noticed that the chair that usually stood in front of my desk had been moved into the corner of the room. The corner was fairly dark due to a burned-out fluorescent light and the closed blinds, but I could still make out the outline of a figure in the dim light. For one wild moment I thought Alan had been released and was back on the job, but the figure in the corner was too large—as in fat—to be Alan.

"Hi, Kate."

He spoke in a whisper, so I didn't recognize his voice. Then he stood and walked toward my desk, emerging from the shadows.

"Stan," I gasped. "What are you doing here?"

He looked like he'd slept in his suit, and his hair wrap had completely unwound. He looked even more demented that usual.

"Waiting for you. I didn't need to wait as long as I thought I would. You got here pretty early. Considering everything that happened last night, I figured you'd sleep in."

I smiled shakily. "That's me; little Miss Conscientious."

"I take it you didn't have a chance to read the paper this morning," he said.

I shook my head.

"Allow me to bring you up to date, then." He produced a heavily creased newspaper article from his breast pocket.

"The caption reads 'County Attorney on the Lam.' The gist of it is that one of the people arrested last night, and I'm taking a wild guess it was Alan, implicated me in ongoing thefts of drug evidence from the sheriff's department."

Stan read the last part of the article. " 'Agents went to the county attorney's home to arrest him, but he was not there, and there were signs in the home that indicated he'd left in a hurry.' "

"The newspapers never get it right."

"You're *not* involved in the thefts then," I said, relieved.

"Oh, but I was. The part in the article about my house showing signs of a hasty departure—that's what they didn't get right. I didn't bother to go home last night. My house is always a mess. As for the thefts from the evidence room, I knew what was going on all along. In fact, I've pretty much run the operation for the past few months."

"But Alan told me you weren't involved," I said. "He covered for you. You should be fine."

"Alan is an egotistical little shit with no guts. You can bet he pointed the finger at me as soon as the FBI put some pressure on him. He's jealous as hell of me. He didn't like playing second in command. For years Alan was our only man on the inside at the county attorney's office. Every so often he managed to slip a few undercharged drug cases through, telling the guys in Charging he was just following the orders of the current county attorney. But he couldn't use that line very often without raising suspicions, and he sure as hell couldn't take the risk of pushing through a misdemeanor charge on a really big case.

"Kenly told me all about the operation one night after we'd shared a few drinks—actually more than a few—at the country club. After that he paid me a percentage of his ill-gotten gains to keep me quiet, but I saw a way to substantially increase the profitability of the operation. I convinced Kenly that if I ran for office and won, we could push through twice the number of cases Alan had been sliding through and double our drug inventory. The sheriff liked the idea too. After all, the county attorney is top guy in the office on charging matters. So Kenly backed me in the election for county attorney, and here I am. I tried to squeeze Alan out since we didn't need his services once I was elected, but the little dick threatened to go public. But he doesn't have the guts for a big operation. When you started asking questions and talking to people, he got scared and overreacted. That's when he went after you and Turner."

Rantwist came closer to my desk. He stared at me with a wild look in his eyes.

I felt the situation was not heading in a good direction. This was immediately confirmed when I saw the gun in Rantwist's hand. He was of course pointing it at me. I figured the more time I could buy, the better.

"What about the overcharged misdemeanors?" I asked hurriedly.

Rantwist giggled. When a man like Rantwist giggled, it was a sure sign that nothing good was going to happen.

"The overcharging was my idea too. I figured my crusade against acts contrary to nature would distract the public and get me a reputation as a righteous law-and-order guy, the last person anyone would think was involved in a scheme to sell drugs taken into evidence. I feel kind of bad about the charges against the flag waver, though."

"The flag waver?" I asked weakly.

"You know, the naked guy on Third and Central."

I nodded. The Larkin case was what got me started on this whole thing, which had resulted in the mess I was in now. I hoped Mr. Larkin would appreciate the trouble I'd gone to for him.

"What are you planning to do?" I asked. The answer was pretty obvious, with him pointing the gun at me and all. But I was running out of small talk.

"I'm planning to shoot you," he answered.

"Why? The most you'll get is some time in prison for the part you played in the thefts. If you kill me … well, I don't need to tell *you*, but this is a death penalty state."

Rantwist giggled again. His giggling unnerved me more than anything— except for the gun.

"Prison time for a county attorney *is* a death sentence. Besides, killing you would make me feel good. I've really grown to dislike you."

He brought the gun's muzzle to within inches of my head.

I pushed my knees up as hard as I could. My desk crashed over onto Rantwist, knocking the gun out of his hand. Thank God for cheap government-issue desks.

I scrambled for the gun. Rantwist scrambled for it too, but I was quicker, largely because I was not wearing a desk. I grabbed it and inched backward toward the door, keeping the gun trained on Rantwist, who had dislodged the desk and was crawling rapidly toward me while emitting a continuous stream of obscenities.

I grabbed the doorknob and pulled. The door wouldn't budge. Then I remembered the doorstop. I leaned down to pull it out, but Rantwist was already at my feet. He flipped onto his back and tried to kick the gun out of my hand. I quickly straightened up and held the gun above my head. Rantwist stood and tried to grab it from me, but I had the height advantage.

"Help!" I screamed.

"You bitch!" he screamed. "You're fired!"

Someone pounded on the door. I tried to kick the doorstop away with my heel, but the little sucker wouldn't budge.

I heard the sound of splintering wood, and the door crashed down on top of me. Everything went dark.

Chapter Seventeen

I was lying in a hospital room when I woke up.

The woman in the bed next to mine was singing what sounded a little like "Puff, the Magic Dragon." Her tone was so off, though, I couldn't be sure.

The singing stopped abruptly in mid-refrain.

"She's awake!"

My vision, which had been a little fuzzy when I woke up, started to clear. MJ's beaming countenance slowly emerged into clarity.

Someone else in the room exclaimed "Hallelujah! It worked."

"What worked?" I asked groggily.

"He just kissed you," MJ chortled. "You weren't coming around, so he said he was going to try the prince charming approach, and it worked."

"Who he?"

"Bryan!"

I rolled my head over to look where MJ was pointing and saw Bryan standing on the other side of my bed with a huge grin on his face.

"What happened to me?" I asked, refusing to give Bryan credit for my miraculous awakening.

"You got doored," said MJ.

"What she means," said Bryan, perching on the side of my bed, "is that when your rescuers broke through into your office, the door fell on top of you. Fortunately, one of them was able to tackle Rantwist before he got away."

"Who were my rescuers?" I asked.

MJ answered. "You're not going to believe it; Beth and Jenny."

"Beth from Rantwist's office, and Jenny from Misdemeanors?" I looked questioningly at Bryan. "Where were you?"

"Hey. Gimme a break. Am I in charge of Kate rescues? I didn't know anything about Rantwist's involvement in the evidence thefts until I got back from walking Ralph and read the newspaper. By the way, that dog's turds are huge. Anyway, I called your office as soon as I read that Rantwist was implicated in the thefts. You didn't answer, so I called Jenny and asked her to go check on you, and then I jumped in my car and headed downtown. In the meantime, Jenny ran into Beth on her way to your office. Beth was bringing you some cookies. She figured you'd need them after everything that had happened. They heard you screaming and banged on the door. Beth recognized Rantwist's voice, as well as his vocabulary, so they backed up and ran full speed at the door, putting their shoulders to it. They took the door down on their second try."

"And after they broke through, they took Rantwist down?" I asked in amazement.

"Actually, Beth was the one who tackled him. I got there pretty soon after, and I had to peel her off of him. She had him in a hammerlock and was pounding his head into the floor. That lady has a lot of repressed rage."

"Beth sent you some cookies, by the way. She feels really bad about the door falling on you."

I looked around the room for the cookies.

"MJ ate all the cookies," he said.

"I didn't want them to go stale," MJ countered defensively.

Both MJ and I were released from the hospital the next day. Mitchie picked up MJ, and, after a brief custody battle between Joyce and Bryan, Bryan drove me home. Ralph was so overjoyed to see me that he came close to knocking me over and sending me right back to the hospital. Bryan, who had assumed dog care duties during my time away, pulled Ralph off me and put me to bed. After he made sure I was comfortable, he went to the kitchen to make some tea to go with the cookies I'd insisted he stop and buy on the way home from the hospital.

Ralph plopped down on the floor next to my bed. I leaned over and stroked the top of his head. The events of the past week had been confusing and terrifying. One thing was clear though: I needed to find another job. I was not cut out to be a prosecutor. I would always reflexively jump to the defense of the underdog, so I might as well accept it and go back to being a criminal defense attorney. I just wished the underdogs were better at paying their bills.

CPSIA information can be obtained at www.ICGtesting.com
Printed in the USA
LVOW040801080112

262878LV00001B/121/P